This story is a work of fictio
places, and incidents are fictitic
to actual persons, locations, or events is coincidental.

ISBN: 978-1-989206-84-3

UNNERVING

RETAIL

RENEE MILLER

For most of my life, murder never crossed my mind. In fact, I've always been a positive, kind person. One of those "wouldn't say shit if her mouth was full of it" girls.

It's hard for even me to imagine now, but it's true. Everywhere I worked, I was a star player. Glowing customer reviews. Coworkers loved me. It was great...for management.

To earn those five-star reviews, I swallowed slights and attacks by at least a dozen people every week for years. I smiled and nodded through rants, tirades, and all out evil villain monologues. I've been spat on, pushed, stared down, and had my chest poked by elaborately manicured nails. For those of you not in customer service, the chest poke is a favorite way for irate "Karens" to put a lowly retail worker in her place. Don't even get me started on the shit I dealt with in my personal life. We'll save that for the therapist I'll never talk to.

And hey, I can admit there've been positive changes in my life thanks to Retail. I can't deny that. I mean, it's helped me find my voice and it's made what I want and don't want very clear. It's also led to angry crying in the bathroom on my breaks, insomnia, and bouts of lying on my kitchen floor, uniform in my hands, desperately trying (and failing) to come up with a good enough excuse to stay home. I got pissed off. Fed up. Frustrated that I couldn't fight back, and (sometimes) a little bummed that my life choices had led me to a place where a stranger thought it was okay to berate and diminish me for just doing my job. Being someone's whipping post is exhausting physically and mentally. I don't recommend it.

Retail sucked the goodness right out of me. I just couldn't swallow one more piece of shit from some yahoo who thinks he's better than me because he's buying what my boss is selling. Some of you might think I had to be unbalanced from the start. I mean, sane people don't kill, right? Mental illness has to be the reason I snapped. Well, it's not. I know right from wrong, and I do give a shit that maybe I've strayed from the morally correct path. It's why I have a code, a set of conditions under which I'll consider killing someone. I don't just target people for the thrill of it. It's not about an adrenaline rush or some twisted sexual fantasy. I've simply had enough and I'm cleaning up the aisles of life by getting rid of these people.

Unbalanced? I guess you're entitled to your opinion, but keep in mind that everyone has a breaking point. Even good people. A line that, once crossed, can't be erased. The laws of society and morality keep us in check for the most part, but occasionally, as in my case, the shit is piled so high, we just can't keep eating it. The only way to get past it is to set it on fire.

As long as you don't get caught.

By the time I got to Valu Mart, the path was set, and my feet were firmly on it. All I needed to become what I am was a spark. It happened slowly. Rather than flaring up as a flame tends to do, it unfolded, little by little, like the petals of a flower, until I saw what I'd been ignoring all along.

I can be the instrument of change. The tool that fixes what's wrong in this industry, starting with the customers of the Valu Mart.

Now, I don't have a usual shift, but it seems I'm almost always working weekends. Most days I'm stocking shelves or manning a checkout lane, but on the weekend I'm the person in charge and my job is basically just running around like a lunatic putting out metaphorical fires and getting shit on by every Tom, Dick, and Karen that walks through those automatic doors. Shit rolls uphill, guys. You think that irate Karen reaming you out over the ten cents you overcharged her is bad? Try being the manager she so desperately wants to talk to. Doesn't really matter where your job is in retail, though. Abuse is abuse. Insults are insults. Threats...you get the idea. I'm surprised more of us haven't taken things postal. Maybe some of you have and, like me, you're so used to cleaning up other people's messes that you've hidden your crimes well. We should talk.

Now, snuggled under my trendy big yarn blanket, crafted by a local woman who also sells scented candles and drinkware adorned with vinyl stickers she printed on her Cricut machine, I struggle to remember a time when I didn't want to kill someone. I know there was one. Long before Covid. Long before the Valu Mart.

She's gone now. The first kill took her and she's not coming back. What remains doesn't look like a killer. Hell, I don't even look like someone who'd throw a punch. The reflection staring back at me from the rain-soaked window looks pale and tired. Sick of other people's bullshit. Tired of feeling like her best isn't good enough.

My grandma used to say that we can't blame other people for our misery. Happiness is a choice. She'd tell us if we don't like our life or if we can't abide how someone is treating us, then stop complaining and do something about it.

Well, she was right. I did something, and I've never been happier. Instead of bad shit happening to me, it's happening *because* of me.

The Member

I've learned that the problem with most people is they want to feel important or better than everyone else. So, when they go into a store or a restaurant, or anywhere someone has to "wait" on them, they develop an attitude. "Customer is always right," they say. No, fuckwad. The customer is almost never right.

We're not going to talk about the moderately annoying people, though. The stories I'm about to tell you are about the overachievers. The Kings and Queens of Asshole. You might think there can't possibly be that many, but you're wrong. I used to think the same thing, and then a pandemic happened and let me tell you kids, humanity is fucking swimming in assholery.

As you can probably tell by now, I'm dealing with a bit of rage. It's hot, thick, and while it cools when I leave work for the day, the second I walk through those doors and utter the words "How can I help you?" it flares up again. It's not consuming me. As I said, I never let emotions dictate my actions. It does, however, fuel my desire to change my situation.

For a long time, I thought there wasn't much to be done about it. I mean, it's my job to take other people's crap. Smile. Be polite. Never snap at them. Never glare. Never, ever point out the fact that they're massive shit-fuckers. Let them call you names, if that's what makes them feel better, let them yell at you, spit on you (yes, it happens), and get the manager when they demand it. Let them bitch, moan, rant, gripe, and complain. It's their right, after all. They're paying for it. You must do all of this for that generous wage they call "minimum." Yay you!

To be clear, I've always wanted to retaliate. I wanted to tell them to go fuck themselves. I wanted to shove things up their asses and down their throats; sometimes both at once. I wanted to quit. I needed the job, though, because I own a house thanks to my dead father, and those don't pay for themselves, so I did as I was told most of the time. I swallowed every ounce of shit they gave me and thanked them for it. Told them to have a great day, even though they ruined my whole week.

Something had to give eventually, I suppose. No one can take that much abuse forever, right? The answer is no, they can't. I took a lot, though. Pretty proud of myself, to be honest. I bent over and got fucked for a long time before deciding it was time to be the fucker.

And then I met a man we'll call The Member. Before we begin with how I reclaimed my...let's call it power, I'm going to tell you about his story, because he is the reason my thoughts turned from "poor me" to "poor them."

He wore a lot of turtlenecks, even in the summer. When he came through my cash the first time, I noticed his penchant for covering up and wondered why he'd cover up a body he obviously worked hard to sculpt, and then I decided he must have a skin condition or horrific scars. Should've been the first clue something wasn't right about him. I'm not a cop, though, so it didn't occur to me that I should care.

The Member, a name I gave him early on, after someone said he was a government official (member of parliament, in case you're wondering, and also a dick, thus: The Member), was tall, not ugly, although his hair had started thinning, and he spoke softly. He always said please and thank you, sometimes asked how my day was going, or mentioned a detail about my appearance ("New haircut?" he'd ask. "Just brushed it," I'd reply, and we'd both laugh awkwardly) and he made eye-contact in a way that made you feel flattered, rather than creeped out. Long enough to know he saw you, but not so long you worried he *saw you.* That's important to note because everyone thinks the crazies are easy to spot. Not so. The dangerous ones are skilled at making a person feel at ease.

Unbeknownst to the entire town, most of whom felt safer knowing this stand-up guy called a place like Tweed home, The Member was a freak show. Like every serial killer, he was smart until he wasn't.

Let's start a little before his mistakes. That summer several female residents reported break-ins. The intruder didn't steal anything valuable, though. He took underwear. Some of it he tried on and left on the bed or the floor, so the homeowner knew her lacy bits had been touched by someone else.

We were nervous about the whole thing, but not scared. I mean, he rubbed his balls all over the things that go right over your lady bits. If you knew he'd been in your house, how could you be sure he only tried on that one pair of underwear? Better to wash everything...or burn it. I mean, gross, right? But at least he was waiting until no one was home and didn't seem interested in hurting anyone. He just liked to wear dirty panties. Everyone's got their kink, I guess.

What we didn't know was that The Member didn't just like women's lingerie, he was *obsessed* with it. This was no mere fetish, kids. He enjoyed its soft texture against his rough skin. He liked the way the lacy edges tangled in his body hair, and how the silky triangles cradled his ball-sack. He liked it so much, he took photographs. Many, many photographs. We didn't know that at the time, but later, we knew more than we ever wanted to. Can't unsee some things, if you know what I mean.

The cops didn't say much about the break-ins at

first. Most of what we knew was through word-of-mouth. This person reported an intruder to her sister, who knows the local server at the pizza place, who told about a dozen customers, who went home and told a dozen more people, and so-on. Small towns are great like that. Thanks to the local law enforcement's silence on the whole matter, we were forced to fill in the blanks ourselves. That should never be allowed to happen, by the way.

"Think he broke into your place?" Beatrice asked me once—the older lady they hired and should've fired months ago. "I think some of my underwear is missing." She grimaced, her cheeks bright pink. "Hope he wasn't in my house."

No, Beatrice, I thought, he didn't try on your yeast-infected G-strings. He likes them young and pretty. Duh.

"I doubt it," I said, smiling as The Member approached her lane. I put three rolls of quarters and a stack of fives into her drawer.

"Doesn't it bother you that we might never know?" she asked.

"Nah," I said, smiling at The Member. "I'd rather not know, to be honest."

I could've said I was the wrong age. Too old. I'm hardly going to admit that, though, am I? And I didn't have teenage daughters that might lure this nut to my door. Really, I didn't care if he had been in my house. If he's that desperate to smell my dirty laundry, have at it. All in all, our intruder seemed harmless. Annoying, yes, but not someone to fear.

"Morning, ladies," The Member said as Beatrice began to scan his groceries.

"Morning," I said and quickly left the registers as Beatrice turned on her charm. Last thing I needed was to watch Beatrice flirt.

We had a few interactions like that, talking about the creeper with the panty fetish, with the Member present in the background, listening to it all. How he must've chuckled at our gullibility. Now I wonder if people like me, who weren't afraid of him at all, angered him or pleased him. Guess it doesn't matter now.

The Member wasn't content with just glamor shots and dress-up for long. Soon, he escalated, as his type tends to do, and started breaking into homes while the women were still present. According to people who know because he recorded his little adventure on his phone and it was played during his trial, the first time he waited for the kids to go to school. Then, brazen as all get out, he walked around the house in broad daylight, after peering into windows to confirm that Mom was in the shower.

Careful enough to make sure the neighbors

weren't watching, a remarkable thing in this town, he walked through the front door, into the living room, up the stairs, past the bathroom door, which was open, but Mom was too busy enjoying some much-needed solitude in her shower to notice the man in her home, and to the back bedroom, where the thirteen-year-old daughter slept. He spent a little time going through her drawers. Found a couple of items he liked in the laundry hamper, and then, when the shower stopped running, he crept across the hall into the master bedroom, slipped into the closet, and waited for Mom to go out as she usually did to run errands.

She didn't leave right away, though. First, she walked through the house naked before dressing slowly, posing in front of her mirror, checking out this angle and that, noting the cellulite developing around her hips with a curl of her nose. Finally, she left the bedroom and went to the kitchen to make herself a tea.

The Member left the closet, picked up the bra discarded in favor of a more comfortable option, and removed his shirt. As he put the bra on, he listened to Mom moving about downstairs, and he became aroused. The knowledge that he might be caught, might have to run or fight...or worse, excited him. The friction of the lace cups over his nipples added to his pleasure. He dropped his pants when the radio came on downstairs, stroked his dick while Mom sang along off-key to Sia's *Chandelier,* and came as the vacuum interrupted her incessant screaming of the chorus.

He wiped his semen on a pretty lilac-colored camisole from the top drawer of Mom's dresser. He then carefully folded it and replaced it before he slipped from the bedroom, down the stairs, and—oh, there's Mom. He held his breath, his erection returning as she walked right past him to the boy's room, with her vacuum in tow.

One...two...three...four...

Safe to go. Quickly, he walked down the stairs, through the freshly vacuumed living room, to the back door this time (Mom would see him from the boy's bedroom window if he went out the front), and outside. Lacy treasures in his pocket, he strode through the neighbor's property with a hop in his step. When he returned to his truck, he had the teenage girl's dirty panties around his wrist and could barely contain his need to view the photos he'd taken.

And that wasn't all he did.

Emboldened by his ability to slip in and out unnoticed, he needed more. It was too easy. He needed a challenge. Not long after his first successful home invasion, he broke into a house shockingly close to his own in the wee hours of the morning. The woman, who lived alone, woke up, as he hoped she would. He wore a mask. Instructed her to do as he said if she wanted to survive. First, he told her to take off her clothes. The rest doesn't bear repeating. When the sun rose, he was gone, and the woman would never recover from what he did.

The thrill he experienced that night, the power he realized he had over another person, the fear he evoked, was like heroin. He couldn't get enough, so he did it again and again.

Still, not much from the cops. No warnings. No big press conference about what happened. Not even a statement to comfort the terrified women who began locking their doors and waking at the slightest sound.

At the grocery store, we heard the details, relayed by a friend of a friend of the victims who was enraged the police weren't issuing any warnings. I guess I understand their logic. Panic wouldn't help anyone. It could get someone killed. Imagine a husband or friend trying to surprise you by arriving unexpectedly. He might wear a baseball bat to the face or a bullet in the gut. Later, after the worst happened, a "source" close to the police said they kept the rapes on the down-low so they could investigate without tipping him off.

Sure...

It wasn't long before the burglarizing and raping became insufficient to meet The Member's needs. He liked feeling powerful. He relished knowing that he held a woman's life in his hands. He enjoyed the fact that when he left them, they'd never be able to erase him from their minds. The chaos he left behind was like an addiction and he needed more to maintain his high. Terrorizing them wasn't enough. Violating them wasn't enough. Breaking them down until they were barely a shadow of their former selves didn't scratch the itch. He needed to own their soul, which, as we've been told by numerous psychopaths in those true crime documentaries, can only be captured at the moment of death.

He started with an acquaintance. She knew him. Trusted him. Had no reason to fear him. He didn't have to break into her house. She let him in. I can't imagine what it must've been like when he showed his true self to her.

Was the plan to kill her all along? I don't think so, but I'm no expert. He played with her, tortured her, and then left her to die. No one suspected a thing, because it was in another town, far enough away that cops didn't make the connection with the serial rapist running around here.

You're probably thinking he's pretty smart. What stupid thing got him caught?

Ego. I know, cliché and disappointing, but there you have it. He believed himself to be untouchable, so eventually, he went hunting in his own backyard. Chose his target. Stalked her. Learned her routine.

Waited for the right moment, abducted her, and he should go straight to hell for what he did after that.

Until this point, he'd made sure to do his dirtiest deeds away from his wife and his personal life. It made it harder to connect the dots, which was important. This time, though, he wanted more time, so he broke that rule. He took her home. Kept her with him for a while. During that time, he didn't try to clean up the evidence, not even after he dumped her body.

That's not what got him caught, though. His mistake was thinking no one could link him to his victims. In his mind, he was above suspicion, so he didn't clean up his crime scene. He left tracks in the mud behind her house and a partial print on her back door. The cops soon realized that only a few people could have left those particular boot prints, so narrowing their search was pretty easy. Thanks to the sharp eye of a cop doing a routine traffic stop, he was caught. While they didn't have a full print, the boots combined with a partial match was enough to convince the cops they had their guy.

A smart killer knows you always leave something behind, no matter how careful you are, and he left a lot, because he wasn't careful at all. When they searched his house, the photos alone were more than damning. He also had videos on his phone and computer and heaps of women's underwear stashed in his garage. The forensic evidence left by his last victim sealed the deal.

I thought the law would take care of him, or at the very least, it'd help some lifer in a maximum-security prison take care of him. But it didn't. They sent him to jail, where he sits in a cell by himself, isolated and protected from the other inmates. Day after day. Was that punishment enough?

I discussed this one morning with Penny, a cashier who is always so damn happy and cheerful, she almost makes you want to drink.

"I heard they reached a verdict," Penny said as I checked the change in her drawer.

"Yeah, so did I," I said. "Life. No parole."

"I heard he's separated from the other prisoners," Penny said. "Solitary confinement, they said."

"Yeah, for his safety," I replied. "It's bullshit."

"Well, he's got life in prison. Don't you think that's enough punishment?"

"For terrorizing the entire town and then raping and murdering innocent women?" I slammed the cash drawer closed after putting in a few rolls of change and some five-dollar bills. "I don't think so. Justice would've been some biker-looking giant of a man fucking him until he bled and then scooping his throat out with a plastic spoon or whatever convicts use for throat scooping these days."

"You're so morbid." Penny giggled. "But good

point. He probably likes being alone."

"Makes me angry to think about how he gets to just keep on keeping on. Sure, he's locked away, but where is his torture? Where is his pain? They protect him in there, and that's not fair. No one protected those women. Why should he get any more than he gave them?"

"Wow," Penny said. "Calm down, Cujo. At least he's not out there still wreaking havoc. I sleep better knowing he'll never get out."

"I guess so," I said to end the conversation. I didn't sleep better. It ate at me that someone like that got better treatment than he gave those women. I obsessed over it for a long time before I was able to convince myself that there was nothing I could do about it. Why waste energy on something I couldn't change?

My thoughts turned to the psychos I encountered at work every day. Their crazy went undetected because they hid it well most of the time. It comes out at the store because they're not afraid to be themselves in front of us. No one actually sees the cashier or the stock boy. They don't think about us at all, so their masks slip.

Then I wondered, what if there are more Members out there? What if they're just one opportunity away from doing the things he did? What if they're planning to do worse? What if they already have and got away with it?

Being invisible, I could get away with it too.

Mama's Boy

His mama was evil. The voices told him so. Robert tried to prove they were wrong. Mama loved him. Hadn't she taken care of him his whole life? When Daddy passed, she protected Robert. Made it look like an accident. How could an evil person do something so good?

"She hates you," the voices said. "Trying to kill you."

When he took his meds, Robert wasn't a bad guy. He also gained about twenty pounds. Robert didn't like being fat, so sometimes he didn't take them. He told Mama he did, though, so she'd shut up. She rarely questioned him. He knew she didn't believe him, but she was afraid of ending up like Daddy. Sometimes, the fear in her eyes spoke volumes. If she loved him, she wouldn't be afraid.

The night she left, Robert had been off his meds for three months. The voices were loud. Almost deafening. They warned him she was up to something. He kept telling them they were wrong. Mama would never hurt him. She might be afraid, but she did love him. He was her boy. Her only child.

But then she said *the thing*.

"Robbie," she said, leaning heavily on her walker. "You can't be saving all this crap." She waved at the stacks of newspapers and pop cans he'd salvaged from his neighbors' recycling boxes. "It's a fire hazard and I can't get through to the kitchen."

"I'll move it to the spare room," Robert said. He couldn't get rid of it. She knew he was building a ship, which would keep them safe when the aliens came. Those pop cans might be in the way now, but when the voices gave him the blueprints to the ship, they'd be the thing that saved their lives.

Mama sighed. "The doctor says I'm getting too old to take care of you."

"You're not that old."

"Well, thank you, but we both know I'm getting up there. I went to see a place today. It's got a pool and a movie room. You'd have your own apartment. It's a lot like you have here, but it'd be all yours."

Robert put the TV remote down. He was careful to keep his eyes downcast. If he looked at her, the rage would come, and he wanted to be patient. Clear. "Mama, those places are for retards."

"No, they're not. Lots of people like you—"

"*Like* me?"

"She's getting rid of you," the voices whispered. "Wants the ship all to herself."

Robert swallowed. "I'm not going."

"They'll be here tomorrow to get you."

"You never loved me," he whispered.

"I just can't keep up, Robbie. I'm too old to be worrying about you and this house. I'll be leaving too."

"Where will you go?

"To that place on the hill. They have nurses and doctors there. It's very nice."

"Kill her," the voices urged.

Robert tried to ignore them, but he found himself picking up Mama's cane. It was hot against the palm of his hand. The voices multiplied and increased in volume until they became a cacophony of sounds. Shrill, almost painful, they blocked out whatever reason remained in Robert's subconscious.

Mama was still talking. Always talking. She didn't see him raise the cane. She felt it, though. Her soft "Oh!" was followed by several screams. Robert didn't stop swinging the cane. She fell to the ground. He kept hitting her.

Again.

Again.

Again.

Blood sprayed his pants. It soaked her nightgown. The floor became a slick pool of her agony. His arm was tired. The muscles ached. They begged him to stop. He couldn't, though. Not until the voices quit screaming.

Mama curled into a ball. Her face, already swelling, was no longer recognizable. Blood gushed from her right eye, where Robert's frenzied movements had jammed the leg of her walker into the tender flesh. As he took this all in, the voices died down to a whisper. Mama didn't move. Her shoulders lifted in a jerky pattern. Still breathing.

"Clean it up," the voices said.

Robert set the cane down and then walked to the kitchen for some paper towels. The voices told him what to do as he went to work. Call the cops when he finished. Tell them he found his mother on the floor. She must've fallen down the stairs. Never used her walker like she should. He looked at the cane, now cleaned of her blood.

"Better if you had the cane," the voices said. "A crippled man could never hurt someone."

That was the day Robert developed his limp. The cane, a trophy and a prop, would never leave his hands. Not even while he slept.

Mama would be okay. She couldn't stay at the house, though. Robert had no use for evil things like her. When the aliens came, they might take exception to his associating with creatures such as Mama, and they'd just take the ship and leave him behind.

He knelt to brush the hair from Mama's face. "Sorry, Mama," he whispered.

—

Well, that's how I imagined the nasty incident anyway,

based on something written online about him. I'm not sure what really happened but let me be clear: Robert wasn't special. He wasn't someone you fucked with, either, because you never know just how far crazy will go. I'd heard the rumors about what he did to his mom. The cops that frequented the store told us what they thought happened, but just couldn't prove. Later, they found a journal he kept that revealed the true extent of Robert's issues, but before I crossed his path, no one really knew what kind of weirdness lurked in his brain.

His mother took the truth about what happened that night to her grave. During the year she lived after losing her eye and the use of her legs, she stuck to the same story: she fell, and Robert found her when he came home hours later. You'd have to fall awfully damn hard, many times, to end up with the injuries she had. I'm not a cop, though. The cops had to have known the truth too, but without her story corroborating what they knew, they couldn't do much, so they put her in a home where Robert couldn't hurt her anymore.

I didn't know any of this when I first noticed him. He was on my radar because he liked to steal shit. The man actually took a single egg from the carton and stashed it in his pants. We couldn't catch him, but every time he was in and lingered near the eggs, we found an open carton with one egg missing. Every time. He stole other things too, but no one wanted to be the one to confront him, so he got away with it.

I wasn't scared of him. Shoplifters irritated me. I didn't like being made a fool of, and that's exactly what they were doing when they took shit right under my nose. If our damn cameras recorded reliably, we might not be such a big target for thieves. They didn't record, so we had to catch the bastards red-handed.

I tried to catch Robert. I watched him for months. Our boss found out about my mission and said I wasn't allowed to confront him. It's too dangerous. Well, fuck that shit. The man walked with a cane, for crying out loud. I had an arsenal of cans and sharp-edged objects on the shelves. If he went bananas, I'd hit him with every single one. It was worth a few bruises to catch him and maybe even put us all out of his misery.

Ida says I'm too obsessed with shoplifters. If the boss doesn't care, why stress about it? She's probably right, but I still want to catch them. I mean, there are *rules* in life. How can we call ourselves civilized if we don't respect those rules? Robert didn't respect rules of any kind, so I couldn't ignore his stealing. If he didn't go to jail for what he did to his mom, he could at least get banned from the store. Truthfully, he deserved worse. If the opportunity presented itself, I wanted to be the one to make it happen. He wasn't going to go to jail like The Member, where he might toil away the hours finding God so he can die with peace in his heart or some stupid shit like that. I knew he was up to more sinister shit than just stealing an egg or two. No one could be that weird and have no skeletons to hide.

A chance to gain more intel on Robert came in the form of a grocery delivery. We only had one person on shift that day with a car. Small town, guys. Most of us walk everywhere. Also, minimum wage. No one can afford a damn car.

Anyway, Leah had the car, so she was nominated to do the delivery. She was young, small in stature, and not really thrilled about delivering anything to Robert's house. So, I, supportive manager that I am, offered to come along.

Robert had moved after his mother's death. Despite his protestations to the contrary, he was mentally deranged, so things like mortgage payments and utility bills were difficult for him to handle. He missed several payments and the bank foreclosed. Now, he lives in an apartment paid for by Social Services near the school. Yeah, good to know such quality humans are close to our children, right?

"You can go in," Leah said as she turned off the car. "I'll wait here."

I shook my head. These kids had it easy, and they were weak because of it. Only way to toughen them up was to make them do the unpleasant shit. It takes a community, right? I wasn't going to let her be a coward on my watch.

"We both go," I said.

"I'm not gonna lie, I'm scared as fuck."

"Man up, Leah. What's he going to do to two of us?"

"We need a plan," she said. "Like, what do we do if he's waiting in there with an axe?"

I laughed. "He's not waiting with an axe. He just wants his groceries."

"Could be a trap. He's so weird, I wouldn't put it past him. Might tie us up and keep us in his bathtub as sex slaves. You ever seen *Human Centipede?*" She shuddered. "I like you and all, but I don't want to be stitched to your ass...or any other part of your body."

"Get out of the car, weirdo, or you're fired."

Leah never failed to amuse me with her outlandish ideas. One time, she had a little bump under her ear. She worried over it for days, working herself into a dither with theories about a tumor that'd take over her brain, making her a raging lunatic before it eventually killed her. It wasn't a tumor, by the way. It was nothing, went away on its own, and she survived.

Other times, she just did a lot of what if kind of games with herself and anyone who'd participate. What if someone robbed us right now? We'd give him the money, clearly. What if the place caught on fire? We'd leave. Duh. What if that guy with three teeth who hits on the cashiers, but never actually buys anything is really a serial killer who eats his victims and he's just sizing up his next meal? We lay off the snacks so we're less appealing than our coworkers who have more meat on their bones.

Anyway, I made her get out of the car and helped her take the groceries from the trunk. In the lobby, we pressed the button with his last name on it and waited.

"Yes?" a voice asked through the speaker.

"Groceries," I said.

"Who is this?"

"We're from the grocery store. You asked for a delivery."

"What'd I get?"

Leah was now hopping from one foot to the other, something she did when excited, upset, or angry. I glared at her, and then opened one of the bags in my hands.

"I've got milk and looks like some eggs. There's a couple of sandwiches, and—"

"What kind of sandwiches?"

I sighed and lifted one of the cardboard triangles. "Egg salad," I said and lifted another, "and turkey."

"Did I get anything else?"

"Case of pop, bottle of olive oil, some bread, and a couple of packs of cookies."

"And?"

Enough of this shit. "We'll just leave them in the lobby if you don't want to let us in. Have a nice day."

Leah dropped the bags without question, but then the door buzzed, letting us inside. I smiled as Leah groaned and picked the bags up again.

"Rather leave them here," she grumbled as we ascended the burgundy carpeted stairs. "Place smells like asshole."

Actually, the building was a mishmash of odors. Asshole, yes, but also lavender, salmon, mold, and I was pretty sure someone had cooked liver in the last few hours. Hard to tell with liver. Sometimes it lingered for days. It might have embedded itself into the burgundy carpeting they laid in the hallways sometime in the 'eighties, so it could haunt whoever was unlucky enough to pass through.

We arrived at his door after walking up four flights of stairs and then a few feet down the hallway of the top floor. Why did a crippled man live on the top floor of his building? Surely, there were apartments available on the ground floor. How'd he even get up there? I'd seen him walk. It wasn't pretty.

I knocked. Footsteps shuffled inside. I heard him stop, touch the door, probably looking through the peephole, and then a chain rattled as he unlocked it. He opened the door about a foot, leaning heavily on his cane and preventing me from seeing inside. I was dying to know what was in there.

"Why are there two of you?" he asked. "There's only one. Only ever one delivery person."

"New policy," I lied. "Had some issues, so no one delivers alone."

"Usually the boy," he continued. "Never a girl. Two girls now. I don't like it."

"We can just leave these here if we make you uncomfortable."

He seemed to consider the idea, but then stepped back. "No. Can't carry them. The boy always puts them away."

I sighed. Rick, the usual delivery boy, said he was weird like this. It was rare for him to ask for deliveries, but when he did, Robert made Rick stay as long as possible, while he talked about some spaceship shit. What Rick failed to mention was the true level of weirdness we'd find inside Robert's lair.

Leah hesitated as I entered.

"Let's go," I whispered.

She groaned for the millionth time but followed me inside. What we found was...disturbing. Stacks of paper everywhere. Not just newspaper, but loose sheets, magazines, and flattened cardboard as well. Some of the stacks almost reached the ceiling. They bent and buckled, leaning into each other here and there. It'd take one good bump to send them all down like dominoes. I really wanted to bump them.

Blue recycling bins lined the wall behind a ripped brown sofa. They were stacked four high and contained hundreds of flattened pop cans. God, I've never seen so many fucking cans in one place, and I work in a damn grocery store. That's not the worst of it, though. Several pails were jammed between stacks of paper and recycling bins. In these pails were pop-can tabs, plastic bottle caps, jar lids, and what appeared to be dirty rags.

Leah and I stepped over the mess as we made our way to the kitchen. The smell of sour milk and something equally unpleasant hung heavily in the air. Like someone farted, but the fart had soured and then grown a layer of mold. I tried to breathe as infrequently as possible, which resulted in a lightheaded feeling that left me even more unsettled.

In the doorway to the kitchen, he'd stacked pizza boxes. God, there were dozens of them. Some still had cheese and sauce covering the outer edges. I imagined that contributed to the mystery odor. He left a narrow gap between the stacks. I knew my ass wasn't going to fit through, so Leah, skinny bitch that she was, won that coin toss easily.

Beyond the doorway to the tiny galley-style kitchen, he'd stashed shoes. Old ones, newer ones, men's, women's, and kids. Why shoes? I mean, the recycling/trash theme was somewhat understandable.

People did that kind of shit all the time. Shoes, though? What was the meaning behind them? Where'd they come from?

"Awful lot of shoes in here," I said.

"Think they're from his victims?" Leah asked.

"Shh," I said, glancing back at Robert, who leaned on his cane near the almost buried dining room table. "Just climb in and I'll pass the shit to you."

She lifted her leg over the pizza boxes. "This is the weirdest place I've ever been."

"Glad you didn't come alone?"

She laughed as she pushed shoes out of her way, so she had enough floor space to stand. "Not really glad about any part of this."

I passed the bags to her, and she began unloading their contents. Thankfully, there were only four. Leah opened the fridge, grimaced, and quickly jammed the milk and eggs inside. She looked at the 12-pack of Pepsi and then the fridge.

"What?" I asked when she looked at me.

"No room for this. Crisper's full of cans already."

"Set it on the floor. Hurry up."

My curiosity about Robert was more than satisfied at this point. He was weird. Mentally unstable. What he'd done to his mother was the result of a tortured mind. I no longer wanted to make him pay for what he'd done. It was clear the man suffered enough just being alive. Now, I wanted out of that place as soon as possible.

While Leah took her sweet time putting the remaining groceries away, I took the opportunity to really look at the rest of Robert's apartment. I might never have seen the weird aquarium had I just focused on the task at hand, but I did, and what happened next happened. So, there you are.

Remember how I said he stole single eggs? Well, inside a large aquarium that Robert had stuffed into a corner of the room on top of a base of National Geographic magazines, were eggs. They were nestled between layers of shredded paper that filled the entire aquarium. He hooked up a heat lamp on top that shone down on said eggs. Christ, there had to be at least fifty eggs in there. Maybe more. Hard to tell.

"What are those?" I asked. What I meant to ask was *Why* are those? but I didn't.

"Eggs," Robert said. "Going to hatch them and have chickens. They'll be invaluable when the aliens come and take me. No food for humans up there. I have to get rid of the weeds, first."

"Weeds?"

"Bad apples. Rotten ones."

"Okay..."

So, the man bought eggs to eat and stole eggs to...hatch. I can't even.

"Not everyone is righteous enough to go when the time comes. I told them I'd take care of those, so they don't have to waste time finding them. Once they're all gone, the aliens will come."

I didn't want to know, but the words left my mouth anyway. "And how are you going to take care of the bad ones?"

Robert looked me square in the eye. "Kill them."

"Oh."

"You're too close," Robert said. He hobbled toward me, remarkably agile for a man who shuffled through the store at a snail's pace. "Don't touch them."

I leaned back as he approached. "I'm not touching anything. Relax."

"Get away from them." He lifted his cane.

"If you'd move, I could get out of here."

He poked my knee with the cane. "Get!"

"Jesus, buddy. Calm down."

"They're mine!" The cane swung downward. "You can't have them."

Now, here's where shit gets foggy. Leah made a weird scream-yip-gasp sound, and then Robert hit my shoulder with the cane. Not once. Not twice. I actually lost count of how many times the man wacked me with the damn thing. It hit my shoulder, my chest, my head, my leg. Fuck, it was like he grew a third cane-wielding arm to beat me with.

Of course, I fought back. I might have punched him. Probably kicked him. I'm not entirely sure how many times I struck him either. Leah told me later that she didn't see it all, as she tried to escape out the other side of the kitchen, which was blocked by a large armoire that weighed three times as much as she did.

Back to Robert. Our boss always warned us to approach Robert with delicate hands. "Be kind," he said. "Never raise your voice or use sudden movements. Just let him do what he does, and he'll leave quietly." Let him steal what he wanted, hurl abuse if he pleased, and loiter for hours in the lobby, creeping out paying customers as he picked through the garbage can or stared blankly at the wall. Sure. Sounded perfectly reasonable.

I said I wasn't afraid of him, and I wasn't before the caning, but in that moment, I feared for my life. Under that fear was rage. Instead of warning us not to upset him, our boss should have said no deliveries to the lunatic, but no. He let us go to this apartment-sized insane asylum. This shit show might never have happened, but that might mean a lost sale. He definitely didn't say how we should handle the fucking hatchery of rotten eggs, so...yeah. This is really all Corporate's fault, as are most things. Everything came down to money with those fuckers.

Robert spewed profanities as he continued to

strike me with his cane. He said a few other things too, but they made no sense. Something about the spaceship and chickens for Armageddon, I don't know. What I know is that I fought hard. Pulled no punches. Gave no mercy. Somehow, Robert tripped (maybe he was pushed) over the coffee table and landed on his back on top of a stack of boxes. He jerked and twitched a little, made a whistling sound in his throat, and then he didn't move at all.

"Is he dead?" Leah asked, abandoning her impossible armoire escape route and leaving the kitchen the way she entered.

"He can't be," I said, taking a step toward him. "It's not like he fell hard."

"Don't touch him!"

"I have to see if he's okay." I didn't want him to be okay if I'm perfectly honest. The man was a menace. He contributed nothing to this world except misery and weirdness. I couldn't let this poor girl know that, though, so I told myself to freak out if he was dead, so she didn't think I was a horrible person.

Leah stayed where she was as I leaned over Robert's prone body. His eyes were open. Blood pooled on the carpet and the box beneath his head. I lifted his shoulder just a bit, and saw that a tall, pointed statue thing was jammed into the base of his skull.

Yikes, right?

"Uh," I said to Leah, trying to keep the smile off my face. "He's definitely dead."

She screamed.

And she kept screaming until I slapped her.

"Hey!" she said, holding her cheek. "What the hell? You make me an accessory to this shit and then you slap me?"

"You need to calm down so we can get our stories straight before the cops get here."

She blinked. "He went batshit. What's to get straight?"

"He did, but how do we explain how I pushed him to his death? I'm not going to jail for this fuck."

"Oh." She stared at his body. "So…like…maybe he was losing it, and he just fell because he was running around all crazy?"

"But that's a lie," I said innocently. "What if they find out I pushed him?"

"It's not like you meant to kill him."

"No." Well, I didn't *not* mean to kill him either.

"We can say you fought back, but that he kept hitting you," she said. "Because that's what happened. Then, he tripped and fell backward. I think considering the state of this place, they're hardly going to view him as an innocent victim and us as evil murderers."

No, they would not. The bad man got what he deserved, and I finally got to know what it felt like to take the life of someone who deserved to die, even if it was accidental. Win-win. Did I plan it? Hell, no. The day had exceeded my expectations. It was hard to keep the sad-scared face on while I called work and then the cops.

Robert the psycho mother-beater and egg stealer was no more.

I did that.

Would I get to do it again?

The Creeper

I became a bit of a legend around town after Robert's demise. I was innocent of any criminal act. The cops saw that right away. In a small town, though, there's always people who gossip or add more to a story than is really there. So, in some versions, I lost my shit, not Robert, and I killed him in cold blood. I mean, it was no secret I hated the guy, so I understand why they might not believe it was an accident. In other versions, I was defending myself, which made me a badass and a person to be admired and/or feared. I liked that version. Leah didn't say much about what happened, but she was quick to point out that I didn't mean to hurt him to anyone who suggested otherwise.

Anyway, after a brief investigation, the cops cleared me, and my boss didn't fire me. His only comment was, "I told you not to provoke him," to which I replied, "I delivered his fucking groceries, Bill." He just shook his head and went back to his game of Solitaire; my hint to get the fuck out of his office.

Another manager, Kendall, laughed when she heard what happened, and then asked if I could do the same for the guy who was her epic pain in the ass. I wouldn't have considered him on my own, but after she mentioned it, I couldn't stop thinking about how he'd made her life hell for more than a decade.

Kendall is a nice girl, although she works hard to make people believe she isn't. Some might call her plain, but I don't think so. No fuss, no muss is her motto, so she doesn't wear makeup or sexy, skimpy clothes. She prefers comfy jeans, loose sweatshirts, and ponytails. That's not to say she's not pretty. She's cute, although she's got a mouth on her that'd make a trucker blush. Just as she doesn't waste energy on lashes and nails and whatnot, there's no time in Kendall's world for flirting or game playing. She's found the person she wants to spend her life with, and she really doesn't look at anyone else.

So, imagine her surprise when this fellow, let's call him Tim, started popping up a little too frequently for her comfort. He'd show up at the store, which is explainable, because everyone goes there every day, and then on her street, which is out of the way for anyone except the people who live there, and then he'd show up at the post office, the drug store, the gym, and the local Tim Horton's. Basically, every time Kendall went somewhere, Tim would show up there too, eventually.

Now, Tim is from a hamlet near Tweed called Flinton. He's less than average; the kind of guy who blends into everything. You overlook him without realizing you've done so. He's not hideous, but he's not attractive either. He's neither tall, nor short. Not fat, but not skinny. His hair is mud brown. Eyes...I don't actually know what color his eyes are, so don't worry about them. During the winter, he wore what we like to call a Flinton tuxedo, which is a plaid jacket and jeans (often dirty). In the spring, he switched that out for a plaid shirt. Same colors: red, black, and grey. When he felt fancy, he switched to the blue, green, and orange plaid paired with a nice pair of Carhartt or Dickies work pants, but only on special occasions.

Tim noticed Kendall years before, in high school. She never noticed him. No one ever did. I guess the stalking was inevitable. He was genetically designed to lurk in the shadows.

Back then, he'd stare at her in class and follow her home, always keeping a discreet distance between them. He just wanted to see her at first. Nothing sinister. She was pretty and he liked pretty things. His love became so intense, though, that everything else faded into the background when Kendall was nearby. She was perfect. Not fluffy and fussy like the other girls. Smart enough to hold a conversation about almost anything, but not too smart. Nerd girls were too weird for Tim. Kendall liked sports too, but she wasn't super skinny or muscular. She had a woman's shape, which he liked. The fact that those soft curves hid such a strong body made him quiver in a strange way. He didn't like the feeling at first, but eventually he came to realize that quiver was the first stirrings of true love.

Kendall was always nice to him when their paths crossed. In truth, she barely saw him. Said hello because she said hello to everyone. Answered his questions because she answered everyone's. Worked with him in science class because the teacher assigned partners. You get the idea.

When they left school, he couldn't see her anymore. For a long time, he spiraled downward. The good job he landed disappeared. His new apartment, car, and everything else he'd managed to acquire thanks to said job followed soon after. Tim had to move back in with his parents because he couldn't function on his own. Barely remembered to bathe himself, much less wash his clothes.

According to a blog he kept, which was mostly rambling, poorly spelled, misogynistic diatribes, it was unfair that good men were forced to be celibate by egomaniacal, slutty women who deserve to be raped to teach them a lesson. Yeah, he was one of those. Anyway, Tim reported in his blog that he contemplated suicide a few times but couldn't find a way that didn't involve immense discomfort in his final moments. Sure, he could take a bunch of pills and fall asleep forever, but those didn't always work. What if someone found him before the pills could do their job? Then he'd have to live with their pitying stares until he did it right.

He was getting desperate. His life had no meaning. Without Kendall, he was like Tom without Jerry, or Mike without Ike. He was incomplete. Maybe a bullet, he decided. Or maybe he'd take his mother's sleeping pills, put a noose around his neck, and let the drugs put him to sleep and then the noose would finish the job.

Finally, the perfect suicide.

Tim got himself ready. Pills lined up on his nightstand. Letter to his mom on his pillow, next to a journal chronicling his journey toward "freedom" and the unrequited love that took him there. Letter to Kendall next to that. He needed a new shirt, though. No one knew for sure if you were stuck with what you wear the day you die in your afterlife. Tim wasn't going to risk wearing something shabby. He wanted to look smart when he met God or whoever waited for him on the other side.

If he hadn't gone to buy that new shirt, this story might never have happened. It would've made my life easier if he'd just punched his damn card and called it a day in his regular shirt, but he didn't. When Tim walked past the post office on his way to meet his mother, who would drive him to Wal-Mart for his new shirt, he saw her.

Kendall.

Alone.

Looking better than ever.

She didn't see him. No one ever did. But he saw her, and his heart leapt upward, where it should be. He stopped. Stood on the sidewalk at the base of the post office steps and watched her leaf through the envelopes in her hands. She tossed one and tucked the remainder in her bag.

He quickly climbed the steps as she headed to the door, and barely managed to open it for her.

"Oh!" she said and looked him right in the eye for the first time in so long. "Thanks."

Tim couldn't speak. Couldn't breathe. So, he just smiled as she walked past him, brushing his arm with hers, and toward her car. He stood there, door open, until she turned at the end of the street, and her car disappeared.

No death shirt for Tim. He found his reason to live.

—

Tim's stalking of Kendall took on epic proportions the second time around. In high school, he followed her through the halls, made sure to show up at games and events she said she'd be at, and once or twice he'd sat outside her house, concealed by the long hedge that divided her property from the neighbor's. He was always careful not to be noticed.

Now, though, the stakes were higher. She *had* to see him. Had to know how he felt. Had to return his love or...he didn't know what he'd do if she didn't love him back. She just had to.

Kendall had moved in with a guy she started dating in high school. Tim never thought the guy would last, but somehow, he hung on to her, and there were rumors that she was pregnant. Sure enough, over the first few months after their reunion, the truth began to show. She moved back home with the boyfriend and their baby. Saving up for a house and a wedding, apparently. His heart broke at first, but then he decided it didn't matter. So, the guy could do what every other guy could do. He couldn't *love* her as much as Tim and that's what counted.

No big deal, he told himself. Once they were together, he'd treat the kid like his own. He loved her that much. Then a year passed, and two. When she noticed him outside her work one night, he waved. She didn't wave back. Instead, she kind of glared at him and got into her car before speeding away.

He had to show her his feelings. She had to understand. So, he waited outside her house every morning. Made sure to say hello as she got into her car, and wave as she drove away.

One morning, her father exited the house with

her. "What's your fucking problem?" he'd asked.

"Nothing," Tim said. "Just out for a walk."

"I saw you standing there for twenty minutes," Kendall's father said. "You've been here every day this week. I see you again, I'm calling the cops."

Tim walked away that day. He didn't even get to say hello because her asshole father stole the opportunity. She didn't try to defend him either. That stung.

Her father was a dick. Tim never liked him. He chain-smoked cigars and said whatever he thought, even if it was offensive. He was also too strict with Kendall. Didn't let her hang out with boys in high school and was always in her business. She still got knocked up, though, didn't she?

Well, Tim didn't heed his warnings anyway. He'd kill the miserable fuck if it came down to it. Instead, he started following Kendall to work, stayed for hours outside, inside, wherever. He followed her when she and the boyfriend moved, then sat outside her new house, on the sidewalk, staring at her bedroom window. She called the cops a couple of times, as you're advised to do when someone is harassing you, but the cops said he wasn't doing anything illegal. Until he hurts or threatens to hurt her, they can't do shit.

Don't even get me started on stalking laws, man. I can't even.

This continued for years. In fact, that baby he was willing to call his own is now an adult. Her younger brother is in high school. Tim never stopped his pursuit, but he did get more careful after a police officer friend of Kendall's warned that loitering near her car at night was crossing a line that could get him into trouble.

The store was neutral territory. They couldn't stop him from coming in as long as he bought something. She couldn't call the cops if he followed her through the aisles, couldn't ignore him if he asked her questions, because that was her job. She was paid to be nice to everyone.

This is a big problem in retail work, by the way. Girls, often kids, are told to be nice no matter what. Smile. Say thank you. Ignore the way that creepy fuck grabs your hand when you try to take his money. Ignore how he comments on your hair, your eyes, your smile, your body. Smile and be polite, no matter how threatening or intrusive his behavior. Let him tease you if he wants by pulling the money away a second before you grab it. Pretend he didn't just put his hand on the small of your back. Definitely don't acknowledge how he brushed his groin against your ass or how his elbow nudged your boobs in the aisle, when there's plenty of room to get by you without touching at all. Let him call you sweetheart and darling. Pretend you're flattered if he asks for your number or tells you what he'd do to you if he were a few years younger (and not old enough to get arrested for said acts).

In other words, let the predators treat you like prey. It's what you're paid for. They should feel special. Important. You're just there to make their shopping experience enjoyable and if acting like a rapist or pedophile is what does it, then so be it. Shut your mouth and smile.

Not when I'm in charge, kids. As with all the girls who work with me, I told Kendall to be rude. Fuck customer service. Don't look at him. Don't smile. Don't even glare. If he still won't take the hint, get out of sight when he comes in. I mean it's not an ideal solution, because no one is telling him to fuck off because his behavior is unacceptable, but if you take the carrot away, the rabbit will lose interest. Find a new source of food, right?

Not Tim. Stubborn asshole was determined as fuck.

The day he got his was the same as any other. He came into the store for the third time, stood in Kendall's aisle, pretended (terribly) to look at canned beans, while he watched her work. After a while, he finally gained the nerve to brush up against her as he reached for a box of rice.

"Hey!" she said. "Back up."

"Sorry," Tim replied, touching her back. "I didn't see you there."

"Like hell you didn't."

"You can't talk to me like that. I'll tell your boss."

Kendall needed the job. She had kids to feed. Bills to pay. If he complained, it was possible Bill would write her up, so she said no more to Tim and escaped to the back room.

"I can't take it anymore," she said to me and a few other coworkers. Tears welled in her eyes and her nose turned pink as she fought to hold them back. "He's everywhere I go. When he comes in here, he's all up in my shit. He just brushed his crotch against me out there and when I said something, he threatened to tell Bill I was being rude."

"What a dick," I muttered. "Don't let him intimidate you. When's the last time Bill actually fired someone?"

"It's not just being creepy," she said. "He waits by my car at night. Just stares at me, but one of these times, he's going to kill me or kidnap me, and no one will know, because the cops won't do shit. I know you said they keep reports filed, but I don't think they even bother to fill one out when I call."

"If something happened to you, we'd all know who it was," I said. "Not that it helps the situation right now. I'm just saying, he wouldn't get away with it."

"Yeah. Well, at least he wouldn't get away with it."
She rolled her eyes. "I mean, I'd be dead, but that's
whatever."

I realized I wasn't really helping the situation. She
became more agitated and distraught with every word.
"Have you tried getting a restraining order?" I asked.
"It's gotta be at least harassment for him to be lurking
around your car at night. If he's still showing up at your
house, I'm sure someone at the police station would see
there's reason to be concerned."

"I wish." She slammed an empty box into the
compacter. "The cops said he hasn't done anything
illegal, so there's no reason for a restraining order." She
rested her head on her outstretched arm. For several
seconds, she just stood there like that, not moving, and
then, finally, she took a deep breath and closed the
compacter door and pressed the green button to crush
the contents.

"He won't kill you," I said. "He's a fucking creep,
but he doesn't have the balls to hurt anyone."

"I'd have believed that a few months ago, but he's
been different lately. More...creepy. I saw him outside
my window again the other night. This time I'm sure he
was jerking off."

"You saw his—"

"No!" She made a gagging sound. "I mean, the
streetlight made it so I could see his shadow, but his

arm was, you know..." She made a jerking motion with her hand.

"Jesus Christ. Did you call the cops?"

"They said he wasn't on my property, so there wasn't much they could do. I tried to get video, but it was too dark to see what he was doing."

That was too much. I mean, honestly. "Stay here," I said.

"I can't hide all day. I've gotta get my cart unloaded before the truck comes."

"I'll do it. You stay. Maybe condense these skids so Bill doesn't get up your ass about standing around. I'll page you when he leaves."

Tim left shortly after I wheeled Kendall's cart into her aisle. I paged her, and she resumed working while I returned to the back room, contemplating how I might help her with the problem that was Tim.

Handy thing, the Pepsi order had arrived just as I imagined possible "solutions" to our dilemma. If I were the type that believed in mystical shit, I'd say Fate stepped in again, helping me toward realizing my purpose. I'm a realist, though. The universe doesn't do anything for you. Sure, it might create situations that smart people take advantage of, but it was up to me to do the heavy lifting. I knew Tim would be back. If the universe really wanted this to happen, it'd make sure Tim's return coincided with me putting the skid onto the sales floor.

Now, skids of pop are usually tall and cumbersome. Most of the time we left it for the boys that came in at night and we focused on the grocery order. That day, we had a full receiving bay and had to get as much out as we could to make room for the afternoon truck, so the Pepsi order, stuck right in the middle of the bay, had to be moved. It made sense. No one would question why I'd move it instead of leaving it for the night shift.

I noticed Tim loitering in the toilet paper aisle and my mind was made up.

"Let's put this out next to the water," I said to Mack, the girl unlucky enough to be working with us in Grocery that day. "We'll break it down a bit once it's out there."

A lot of heaving, pushing and swearing got the skid through the floppy doors and onto the floor. Then we had a bit of a problem. The skid was almost too wide for the spot I'd cleared, and because someone stuck a stack of chips on one side, and a rack full of Valentine's Day chocolate on the other, we couldn't maneuver the damn thing enough to get it in.

We stood there, eyeballing the slot. "It'll fit if we could just turn the edge a fraction of an inch," I said, knowing full well it wouldn't.

I hadn't seen Tim during the time it took to drag

the skid out, but he'd returned. He always did when Kendall hid in the back. He'd peer through the small windows in the floppy doors just to get a glimpse of her. I bought some time with my lack of spatial sense, and about twenty minutes after we realized we had to move the water and the chocolates, Tim appeared behind the meat bunker, next to the bacon, watching as Kendall wheeled a cart of soup from the back room toward her aisle. She saw him too, and her face lost all color.

If I doubted my intentions before he approached, and I didn't, the fear in her eyes in that moment made my decision concrete. It was unacceptable to force her to live this way. After years of trying to do the right thing, avoiding him at all costs and telling him outright more than once to leave her the fuck alone, he still tormented her. What if she was right and he did get her alone one day? What if one night, after closing when she was all by herself, he hid *in* her car instead of near it? No one would know and I imagine he'd make sure no one could prove anything should he decide to take it that final step and kill her.

Enough was enough. I watched him watching her and an idea came to me that was so brilliant, I almost cried. Keeping an eye on him, I slipped through the doors and picked up the phone. "Kendall to Receiving," I said. She almost ran toward the doors.

"Thanks," she said as she walked past me and

around the corner. "This is getting ridiculous."

"Getting?" I said to myself because she was already gone. "It's past that."

Tim moved closer to where I was, almost inside the doors, but not quite, which was exactly what I wanted him to do. He was so predictable. So obvious. Pathetic, really.

I slipped past him, back to the skid of Pepsi, which we'd set down just a few feet from where he stood.

"Here," I said to Mack, who, trooper that she was, was still trying to find that fraction of an inch I told her would change everything. "Let me try something."

She looked a little skeptical. I wasn't supposed to run the jack, because I'm accident prone, but I was the boss so she couldn't stop me.

Now, these skids of pop were generally built so they won't topple over if they're moved properly. However, if you unwrapped the top rows, maybe accidentally slid your knife through the plastic on the sides, just here and there, and if you pulled the jack out a little, so the prongs were just behind the center board on the underside of the skid, the whole thing might tip. Knife in hand, I walked around the skid, allowing the blade to pierce the plastic in several spots before returning to the jack. I pulled it out quickly, so Mack didn't see what I was up to. Then I tried to pump it upward. "Hey, Mack," I said. "It won't go up."

Mack, a sweet kid who didn't deserve what I was about to involve her in, took the jack from me and pumped it several times. Tim still stood by the doors, about a foot away from the front of the skid, invisible to Mack, because he was tucked into a corner that customers weren't supposed to be in.

I "tripped," so my shoulders slammed with as much force as I could muster into the upper section of the stack. I smiled as it tipped. Too late, Mack tried to correct what was happening. She panicked, pulling back on the jack while trying to lower it. It slammed down to the floor and then lurched forward. In a matter of seconds, Tim was buried under a mountain of pop.

"Shit," I said and grabbed the jack from her shaking hands. "I think there's someone under there."

"Oh no," Mack whispered. "Oh fuck. I knew I shouldn't let you use the jack. The only luck you've got is bad."

"Thanks," I said as I shoved the jack as far into the pile as I could.

Cans at the bottom of the stack exploded. Pop sprayed in every direction. People laughed, but the amusement was quickly replaced by concerned murmurs as I suspect they noticed a body part or two belonging to Tim poking out from beneath the mess.

It required a lot of effort to keep the delight off

my face. A crowd began to gather at the Deli, so I had to be stealthy in what I did next. I shoved the jack into the edge of the almost empty skid. Pumped three times, and then pushed it forward. The pile on top of Tim's body grew taller as the remaining cases of pop emptied off the skid. I dropped the jack, shoved it through the bottom of the skid, and pumped three more times. As I pushed again, I felt something hit the prongs of the jack. It was Tim's head; in case you're wondering, although I didn't know that at the time. I hoped for a rib or a leg at best. Maybe even his back. I shoved it one more time, felt the resistance of his body, and then pulled it back.

"Someone's under there, dear," a lovely old man said. "See?" He pointed.

"Oh shit," I said, covering my mouth to hide my grin. "Oh no."

Hal emerged from the meat room, took one look at me and then the mess on the floor, and into action he went. "Help me move these," he said to anyone who might be listening. He dragged the jack out of the mess and then went to work tossing pop cases aside.

We all pitched in; me, Mack, and even a few customers. As soon as the floor was clear of the mess, everyone gasped. You couldn't miss him lying there, or the blood that blended in with the pop puddle on the floor.

"Call nine-one-one," I told Kendall, who stood at the doors, mouth slightly open. "Tim's...he got hurt."

She smiled a little, but then realized the severity of the situation and took her cellphone from her pocket while Mack and I unburied the creepy fuck who deserved whatever injuries he sustained in the whole event.

When we uncovered what we thought would be his head, we found his feet. Oops. We tossed pop around until he was freed from the mess. God, what a nightmare...for Tim. His nose was bent to the side, blood smeared across his eyes and chin. He wasn't dead, but he didn't look good.

"Help is coming," I said to him and then leaned close enough that he could hear me whisper, "Next time, when a girl says she's not interested, you leave her the fuck alone."

The paramedics and the cops came. They took him away. Witnesses relayed that he was hidden next to the door. No way could me and Mack see him there. A terrible accident.

Tim never spoke or walked again. He wasn't in a coma, but for all intents and purposes, he was gone. I went to see him in the hospital before his parents moved him to a facility for people like him. He could move his eyes and sometimes his fingers twitched, but he couldn't speak or move his limbs. There was considerable debate over whether he was essentially brain dead, but his mother insisted her boy was in there somewhere.

I didn't say anything. I could tell by the way he looked at me, though, that he was fully aware of everything, and he *knew*. Smiling, I set the bouquet of flowers we all pitched in to buy on the table near his bed, adjusted the card that told everyone they were from the staff at our store, and patted Tim's leg before I left.

Not every bad guy deserves death.

The Homewrecker

In a small town, too many negative things happening to you will start rumors, so I had to dial it back after Tim. Mack wasn't wrong when she said I was unlucky. I got all the weirdos and rejects on my shifts. Every breakdown, blowup, and shit show that could possibly happen seemed to happen while I was in charge. So, to ensure no one noticed that death also seemed to follow me around, I had to be extra kind to everyone. Smile more than usual. Give them no reason to suspect that I might not regret the terrible things I was "accidentally" a part of. Robert, it could be argued, was self-defense. I mean, I didn't like the guy at all, but I also didn't set out to hurt him. It just worked out for the best.

Like Dexter, I felt like the universe was on my side. Why would dishing out Karma be so easy if cosmic forces weren't rooting for me? I'm not stupid, though. Law enforcement isn't keen on vigilantes, and assault was assault in their books, no matter what the reason. Tempting fate too much usually got a person arrested.

My ego would never get so inflated that I allowed such a thing to happen to me. I was smarter than The Member and his kind.

I was cleared of wrongdoing in the Tim accident. His blog was discovered, as well as his journal and various "keepsakes" he'd stolen from Kendall over the years, it was determined that in his desperation to see her, he stood in an area that was clearly marked as "Employees Only" and his slightly crouched position made it difficult for me and Mack to see him from behind the skid of pop. The cops totally understood how such an accident could happen. Thank God Kendall filed those police reports when he showed up outside her window several times last year. He might not have been charged, but the incident reports had been kept. He was a creeper, and no one gives a shit about creepers. They barely investigated the incident, which was fine by me.

My boss, though, was worried about future lawsuits, banned me from using power jacks and, strangely, ladders. I was cool with that. Skids are heavy, hydraulic lifting equipment or not. He also gave me and Mack a holiday. The stress of witnessing horrific accidents could lead to PTSD, and he didn't want to be on the hook for future compensation claims. So off I went on paid leave, to lay around my house for two weeks. They also forced me to go to therapy. Four sessions. Dr. Feelings deemed me sane and the whole mess was soon forgotten.

The time at home didn't improve my homicidal thoughts. Instead, I became obsessed with the idea that maybe my hands were touched by God, or whatever it was that kept this old rock turning. Of course, I'm not a crazy person. Dr. Feelings confirmed this. So, I quickly deduced that I wasn't God-touched. Maybe it was just a simple calling. You know, like teaching or medicine, I had a natural ability for doing the shit no one else wants to do. Taking out the trash if you know what I mean.

The problem, I decided as I binged a Ted Bundy documentary on Netflix, was that I hadn't actually killed anyone on purpose yet. It's different when you can explain away what happened, or when they survive as Tim did. It's easy to live with yourself, because you didn't truly set out to take a life, right? Right. To know without a doubt that this was my destiny, I had to kill with intent. Cover it up so it was a secret between me and God. Only then would I be able to say I was meant to do it.

Could I go that far? Would I need to? Maybe it was enough to just punish them as I punished Tim. Hurt them enough that they weren't a danger to others anymore, but don't kill them. Did I really have to take a life? No, I didn't. Did I want to?

The idea terrified and thrilled me.

Accidents are easy to arrange. Easy to make people believe. However, the victim of said accident might see something that incriminates me. If they survive, they can talk about it. Talk about *me*. That left me open to accusations, lawsuits, possibly jail time, and if I'm totally honest, I *wanted* to kill someone. To myself, it was okay to admit that. I wanted to know if it really felt like the serial killers in the documentaries describe.

On the other hand, I didn't want to go full crazy train either. I mean, the thing most serial killers who've been caught have in common is their descent into madness after the first couple of killings. They allowed themselves to spiral to a point where no amount of killing was enough to satisfy the bloodthirsty lizard in their brains. They get drunk on their imagined power, become arrogant, lose touch with reality, become unnecessarily cruel, develop trademark shit, and then they make mistakes. Never give yourself a trademark. I mean, talk about begging to be caught, right?

And unlike most homicidal maniacs, I wasn't interested in killing anyone who'd done nothing wrong. I mean, going out and seeking a victim based on their appearance or gender or whatever was just stupid. Those people deserve whatever they get for being so goddamn basic. I also didn't want attention. It's fine if no one links one death to another. Preferable, actually. I didn't need accolades or fame. Those things always came with handcuffs and lethal injections. No thank you. I'm good without that shit.

I just want wrongs to be righted. I want

vengeance for all those suffering in dead-end jobs in the service industry. That means I only kill when it's deserved. There's a sort of righteousness in that, even if it doesn't fit with our laws or societal morals. Sometimes you've gotta break shit to make progress.

So, about half-way through the documentary about a guy who tortured cats before moving on to people, I decided I wouldn't search for victims. If the universe sent someone my way who didn't deserve to live, then I'd deal with them. If that never happened, so be it. I wasn't a psychopath, so I wouldn't behave like one. I also stopped watching the documentary when I started thinking too much about those poor cats. People killing is whatever. Start talking about helpless animals getting hurt and I'm out. I can't even think about it.

Several months passed with no sign. Sure, people annoyed me, but if annoying got you killed, there goes half the planet.

And then Jolene came into my life. Yes, it's a pseudonym. I'd never put the names of my victims in writing. I'm smart, remember?

On the surface, Jolene seemed like a nice person. She did good things in the community, and she was always friendly on the surface. You could see, though, in her eyes, that she wasn't genuine. Something ugly lurked beneath the surface. I wasn't sure what that was at first.

Jolene, not really a "shop local" kind of girl, suddenly started coming into the store almost daily. I didn't know much about her, nor did I care to before this. I mean, I knew she existed. The town's Facebook page always had posts by her informing people of community dinners, fundraisers, and other events. As I mentioned, she didn't shop local very often, which is a sin of sorts, but it's not one you should die for. I mean, I can admit our prices are kind of outrageous.

The problem with Jolene arose when, after the first week of daily trips into the store for this or that, she began seeking me out. "Hey," she'd say as I unloaded a cart. I'd look up, smile, and continue working. She'd hover for a bit, poke at a bottle of this and a box of that, and then slowly, awkwardly, wander away. It happened several times before I decided she was waiting for something from me. I learned what that was eventually, but at first it was just weird and confusing. I'm awkward enough on my own, I don't need someone helping me along. Know what I mean? I wished she'd just go back to shopping in Belleville.

"Busy, huh?" she said a few weeks into our bizarre courtship.

I faced the tampons and pads while doing my best to pretend I didn't hear her.

"How's it going?" she asked.

"Oh, you know," I replied. "Living the dream." I mean, I'm on my knees on a dirty cement floor, arranging feminine hygiene products on a crooked shelf that made the rows tip over if they weren't stacked just so, making inane conversation with people I barely know and generally don't like, for minimum wage. How'd she think it was going?

She stayed long enough to enjoy a few seconds of awkward silence and then left. I watched her walk away and resisted the urge to follow so I could ask her what the fuck she wanted from me.

After about a week of hellos and shit, she turned back to me after our greeting and said, "You're Jack's girlfriend, right?"

"Um," I set the half-empty case of condensed milk on my cart. "Yes?"

"We used to date in high school."

Jack dated everyone in high school. And what, bitch?

I didn't reply. Instead, I offered a fake smile and opened a case of Duncan Hines vanilla cake mix. The edge of the box nicked my thumb. She waited as I cursed almost silently. What the fuck did she want? Good for her. She dated Jack. Not exactly a prize-worthy achievement. He used to be a slut. Anyone could get his attention back then. He told me he fucked his friend's grandmother once, just to know what it'd be like. I know, I haven't exactly picked a winner, but he's got skills I haven't found with anyone else, and he lets me be me without insisting on labels and shit. We're not even Facebook official, and he's cool with it.

"We met up again at Tammy's birthday party this summer," Jolene said. "It was like old times. He hasn't changed much."

"Oh yeah?" Jack hadn't changed a bit, except for the lack of hair and the beer baby in his belly.

I never went to Tammy Baker's parties. Lots of sitting around, drinking, and little else. I had better things to do than sit in someone's backyard, drinking semi-cold alcohol, while getting eaten alive by mosquitoes. Sleep was far more satisfying for me. Jack loved those things, though, so I happily sent him on his way whenever an invite came. I was also big on personal space and alone time.

"You guys been together long?" she asked.

"Six years," I said.

"And you're not living together yet?"

Her game of twenty questions was beginning to annoy me. I set the box stained with my blood on the floor next to my cart and looked at her. "No, we're not living together. Why do you care?"

She shrugged as she examined a package of chocolate chips. "Just curious. I thought he'd be married with kids by now."

"Well, he might be. I don't ask what he does when he's not at my house."

She laughed.

I picked up my knife and sliced open a case of baking soda.

"So, you guys are in an open relationship then?" she asked.

"No." What the fuck was wrong with her? Who even asks this kind of shit?

"Oh." She set the chocolate chips back on the shelf and then smiled at me. "Well, have a good day."

Off she went, leaving me to wonder what the fuck happened at that party.

After that, I became a little obsessed. I'm not the jealous type, but when a girl starts aggressively poking the bear, it's customary to ask questions. Jack can do whatever Jack wants. There's no rings on our fingers, after all. However, we did agree to be exclusive. *He* insisted and I saw no reason not to agree. I wasn't interested in fucking anyone else, so why not? If he ended things tomorrow, I'd probably be disappointed, because I put a lot of time into him, but I'm not sure I'd be devastated. I was not a fan of looking like a fool, though, so I had to know if there were secrets being kept.

I asked around about Jolene and learned some interesting facts. The good thing about working in a place the whole town frequents is that we get all the gossip. No one person knows it all, but we have access to enough people that know a little, so we can almost make a complete picture of most situations, should we feel the need to put the pieces together.

Jolene was a serial "other woman." She seemed to like stealing men from previously okay relationships. I know, the worst kind of offender. I mean, if you'd betray your own gender, what the fuck are you?

She also liked to befriend the woman she was betraying. In one case, she was friends with the girl for more than five years. They went on trips together, Jolene babysat their kids, and fucked the husband the entire time. Who does that? She's not even that pretty. I mean, she's not ugly, but her eyes are spaced too far apart, and her hair is frizzy. Too much bleach. She drew her eyebrows on, and not very well, and she had a bit of sploosh in her belly. I think, if I were a guy looking to cheat, I'd trade up. Make it worth the effort, right?

"Well," Melanie, my friend of many years, said when I mentioned Jolene's audacity. "I mean, it's really on the guy, though, isn't it?"

"What do you mean?" I asked.

"Sure, Jolene fucks them, but she's not the one who made the commitment. The guy did. I'd say he's most in the wrong. You can't really blame the other woman."

She had a good point, but it didn't free Jolene from responsibility. "But if she's intentionally looking for men married to her *friends*, then she's worse than the guys, because she's trying to break up a home and betraying the most important rule in girl code. Sometimes a guy isn't even thinking about cheating until a person applies the right amount of pressure at the wrong moment."

Melanie nodded. "Yeah, I never really thought about it like that. Why are you asking about her anyway?"

I shrugged. "She was just asking about Jack. Made me wonder."

"You think he's fucking her?"

"Could be. I don't know."

"You should've let him move in," Melanie said. "He's practically begged you."

"It's my house." I know I'm ridiculous about the whole personal space thing, but my father left me the house, not Jack. I pay the taxes and I fix whatever breaks. Why should he just get to move in? If shit goes south, then I'm stuck with kicking him out. If he doesn't go quietly, then it might cost me money as well as time. No thanks.

"I love you," Melanie said. "But you're so weird."

"Thanks. I work hard at it. By the way, not letting him move in doesn't make it my fault if he did fuck her."

"I didn't say that."

"It was implied."

"I just meant maybe he feels unappreciated. If he thinks you aren't that into him, he'll get tired of the relationship eventually."

"I get into him, or he gets into me at least three nights a week. Sometimes more. You're married. How often do you and Ivan get into it?"

She rolled her eyes. "It's not about the sex. It's about the connection. Feeling loved and needed emotionally."

I almost threw up in my mouth. "Still not my fault if he's fucking around. I've been honest from day one with Jack. I'm not into marriage. Maybe down the road I might be, but no guarantees. Even if I wasn't, if he doesn't like how shit is, he should get out of the relationship before sticking it in someone else."

She put out her cigarette and stood. "I can find out what's up if you want. Just remember, you can't un-ring a bell."

Oh, Melanie. So wise. "I need to know if I'm wasting my time with him. If they're fucking, I'll just end it."

"And Jolene?"

"She'll get hers. Karma, right?"

Melanie walked toward the door. "If I were you,

I'd let her think I was her friend, even if you find out she is fucking him. Steal her thunder."

Interesting. "How does that steal her thunder?"

"I think she enjoys the drama, so if you make friends and then don't freak out when it's all revealed, she'll be disappointed. Kick his ass to the curb and don't give her what she wants. Sure, it sucks, but at least you'll have the satisfaction of taking the high road."

The high road is overrated. Not worth travelling, in my opinion. Being her friend was an interesting concept, though. Make her trust me. Get close to her. Then do whatever the universe decides I should do.

And the idea kept rolling around in my brain. I found myself inviting Jolene out for drinks. I texted her here and there. Invited her to a barbeque at my house, making sure Jack was there so I could watch them together.

Oh yeah, they were banging. No doubt about it.

Jack was unusually attentive. His voice got an octave higher when we talked while she was nearby, and he kept looking around like he expected an anvil to drop on his head or something. Jolene, though, played it cool. If I based my suspicions on her behavior, I'd never suspect a thing.

The question was, did someone deserve to die for being a scumbag?

Let's be real for a minute; I desperately wanted to know what it felt like to murder someone, so Jolene never stood a chance of surviving this, even if I acknowledged the fact that adultery wasn't a sin terrible enough to warrant dying.

After the barbeque, I put Jack on notice. I told him I knew he was hiding something, and I needed space to think things over. He was more upset than I anticipated, which was kind of satisfying. Maybe after this was all over, we could work shit out. I might just pretend that I don't know anything and let him run circles trying to make up for the wrongs he did. Maybe. He could die too. I'd decide when I knew how it'd be to kill someone I didn't care about, because I was pretty sure killing someone who meant something to me would be much harder.

Unlike the psychos from movies, I didn't plan Jolene's murder. No sane person does that shit, and I am very sane. Instead, I plotted to the many ways I could cover it up, should it happen, and then waited for the moment to present itself.

It happened after a particularly awful Sunday at work. I got reamed by a woman who seemed irrationally angry about an incorrect tag on our shelves.

"I bought this yesterday," she said waving a bag of cat treats. "And the tag said it was three-ninety-nine."

"Okay," I said.

She waved a receipt. "I paid four-twenty-nine."

Oh my God! She paid thirty cents too much! Call the law.

"I'm sorry," I said. "I'll give you a refund."

"That's not the point," she said. "It's illegal to advertise one price and charge another."

"It wasn't intentional, but whatever."

Now, what some of you may not know is that in this country, it is *not* illegal to put the wrong tag in front of a product. Stores are not obligated to give you the lower price if the price was a mistake, but most do, because they like to keep customers happy. If the price is advertised somewhere, though, or the store guarantees in their promotional material to honor the lowest price, they have to because that's like bait and switch shit, and *that* is illegal.

Anyway, there's also a voluntary program called the scanner price accuracy program. If a store is part of this program, there's an annoying little bonus that customers get if a product is priced incorrectly. If the scanned price is higher than the shelf or advertised price, the lower price will be honored. I mean, of course, right? But there's more. If the correct price is ten dollars or less, the item is free. If it's more than ten dollars, the store must discount the price by ten dollars.

However, we don't do any of that if the customer

doesn't know about this little loophole. They have to ask, and cashiers are told not to speak a word of it unless they do. Guess the cat's out of the bag now, eh? Every time a person points out a mistake in pricing, I hold my breath and wait for the "You have to give that to me for free," spiel. Most don't know about the ten-dollar maximum rule, though. Boy, is that a fun thing to explain when they don't get that twenty-dollar item for nothing.

This woman didn't know about any of it, so she only demanded her thirty cents back, after arguing a bit over the legality of accidentally putting the wrong tag up. I obliged, apologizing politely as I did so. Truly, I was the picture of remorse and regret as I dealt with her. She continued to rant about how every time she came into the store, she always found a sale price that rang up the original price.

Because you look for it, you fucking cunt, I thought. Out loud, I said, "Well, we don't control that. The prices are put into the computer by Head Office. They send us the tags and we put them out. If they've made an error, we aren't aware of it until we scan the items at the register."

"Then you should check the tags before putting them out," she said.

"They send us thousands of tags every week," I said, handing her a quarter and a nickel.

"So?"

I stared. Not worth it. Don't say anything more.

"I'm getting tired of having to check my receipt against the flyer every time I shop here," she said.

I bet you'd check it anyway, asshole.

"Sorry about that," I said as I walked away.

That was the nine o'clock asshole ripping. At one o'clock, an older lady, late sixties maybe, came to the registers, demanding she get yogurt and Doritos for half price. Of course, the cashier called me to talk to her, because that's the glorious perk of being a manager.

"What's up?" I said, knowing nothing good was up just by looking at the woman's sour face.

"I'm sick and tired of the age discrimination in this store," the woman yelled. And I do mean *yelled*. The whole store and probably the people across the street could hear her.

"Uh." I laughed a little because this had to be a joke. "Age discrimination?"

"These multi-deals. What am I, a single old woman, going to do with two containers of yogurt or two bags of chips? I only need one of each. I can't eat more than that. Why should the deals be reserved for families only? Why am I, a single, *old* woman being punished? It's my right to live alone without kids, you know."

"So, just buy one of each." I truly didn't know what she wanted from me. The cashier's expression was one of mild panic. Clearly, she'd already suggested this solution and it didn't go well.

"No!" the woman screamed. "I will not be ignored!"

Yikes.

She slammed a container of yogurt and a bag of Doritos in front of me. "I want these for half price. Just because I can't eat both doesn't mean I shouldn't get a deal too."

"Well, yeah, it kind of does mean that, because the deal advertised is based on purchases of two or more."

"I want it for half price."

"Look, even if I gave you the deal, it's only a discount of fifty cents when you buy two, so you are definitely not getting those for half price."

"Unacceptable. I've complained countless times, but no one is doing a damn thing about it. Who do I call?"

"There's an email for Head Office—"

"I want a phone number and a name."

I took a breath. God, I wanted to punch out her dentures and then shove them up her wrinkled ass. She didn't even deserve those fucking Doritos. Instead of losing my shit, though, I calmly printed a receipt, pointed to the number on top, and wrote my boss' name on it. "This is the owner. Call tomorrow morning and ask for him. He'll be able to tell you who to talk to."

"Well?" she said taking the receipt.

"Well, what?"

"I'm waiting for you to change the price."

"I already told you you're not getting those for half price."

"Bullshit!" she yelled. "I will not be ignored again!"

I thought Robert was crazy, but I was clearly mistaken. "I'm sorry that you're upset, but I only have to honor the sale price and terms, unfair or not. If I gave everyone who screamed at me whatever they wanted, we'd never make any money, and the store would close."

By now, customers had started gathering near the door, enjoying her tirade a little too much. I glanced at the next register. The man paying winked at me. Real funny, dick-smack.

"What am I going to do with two yogurts and two bags of chips?" she asked. "I'm one single, *old* woman."

We get it, lady. You're single and you're old and you're clearly bitter about it. Fuck off.

Sighing, I lifted the chips. "The best before date on these is a month away," I said and then picked up the yogurt. "This expires in two weeks. I suggest, if you want the deal younger, married people with children are getting, you buy two of each. You can eat one this week, and the second next week. That saves you from having to come here again for two weeks. Longer if you make the chips last a month."

She said nothing for a moment, clearly confused by my logic.

"I'm busy, so..." I started to leave the register.

"This isn't over!" she called after me. "I'm sick and tired of being discriminated against. I won't stand for it. It ends now. I want your name. What is her name!"

I kept walking. What a whackado, right?

It was then that Jolene texted me. She had something she needed to get off her chest.

I smiled as I replied. I was in the perfect mood for her confession. "I'm off in an hour," I replied. "Coffee?"

—

In our texts, I asked Jolene to meet me at Tim Horton's, but when she arrived, I told her she'd have to follow me home, because I left a candle burning and the very idea of a fire left me unable to focus on anything else. She bought it. Idiot. As if I'd leave a candle burning. Fire is probably the only thing that scared the shit out of me.

As I mentioned before, I didn't plan ahead. The problem with waiting for unseen forces to decide your next move was that you had to act in the moment. I arrived at my house before her and as she parked in my driveway, I realized that I'd have to get rid of her car and hope no one noticed she was there. The universe would probably help with that too. If this was my calling, it wasn't too much to ask.

I spent a couple of minutes wondering how I'd do it. I had knives. Those would do the job, but the mess didn't appeal to me, so I searched the cabinet beneath the sink. Rat poison might work. How long would it take, though? I couldn't let her leave and die somewhere else.

Then I remembered the sedatives the doctor prescribed in case I lost sleep over the Tim incident. I hadn't taken a single one. I heard Jolene's car in the driveway as I crushed the pills into dust and then quickly swept them into my palm so I could dump them into her coffee.

She knocked twice and then walked inside. Rude. "Hey," she said. "You home?"

"In the kitchen," I replied.

We sat at the kitchen table. I set her coffee in front of the chair that was against the wall on the back side. Nowhere for her to run from that position.

"Cream or sugar?" I asked.

"Sugar, please."

I got a spoon from the drawer next to the sink and the sugar from its place next to my coffeemaker and set both in front of her.

"So," I said after she added three sugars to her coffee. "What's on your mind?"

The light from my kitchen window really highlighted the years on her face. Lines marked her forehead and around her mouth, and she had a faint dusting of lady beard under her chin. Another five years, at most, and she wouldn't be wrecking any homes. The fact didn't make me feel merciful. Opportunity knocked. I had to answer.

"Uh," she traced the rim of her coffee cup with her thumb, "I don't know how to start this."

"At the beginning?"

She laughed. "Yeah, um, so you know how I told you I met Jack at that party?"

"Yes."

"Well...you're probably going to hate me."

I rolled my eyes. "How could I hate you?"

She shrugged, looking down at her cup. "I—well we, me and Jack, had sex that night."

"Okay."

She looked up. "You're surprisingly calm about this."

Disappointed? I smiled. "It's not shocking. I mean, Jack can be impulsive, especially when he's drunk. I'm sure you're not the first. Probably won't be the last."

She scowled. This was obviously not going the

way she hoped it would.

One time was hardly a homicidal kind of sin, but I knew it hadn't been just one time. She hadn't taken a sip of coffee yet. We couldn't continue until she drank it. I'd have to force it down her throat if she didn't do it on her own.

"Is that it?" I asked.

"Pardon?"

"You fucked him at the party? Is that all?"

"No." Now she perked up. "We slept together a few more times after that, but we stopped when you and I became friends."

"Oh," I said. "Was it you or Jack that decided to stop?"

"I dunno." She took a drink of coffee. FINALLY. Another sip. Dramatic pause. A third sip.

"Jolene," I said. "Did you or Jack stop it?"

"He said he felt like it was a mistake."

"So, he ended it."

She drank more than half the coffee while forming her reply. I wanted the answer, but I also wanted her to ingest as much of the sedative as possible, so I waited.

"He brought it up," she said finally. "But I could tell he didn't really want to stop."

I smiled.

"And I care about him a lot, but I didn't want to

hurt you, so I agreed we should end it before things got too complicated."

Lying bitch. I'd already heard a few conversations from Jack's side, and I read some texts on his phone. He ended it because he regained his common sense, and *she* tried to keep it going. She was pretty relentless and threatened to tell me about it if he didn't continue to fuck her. To his credit, Jack stood firm. He said he loved me and made a mistake with her. If part of making amends was coming clean, so be it. Apparently, Jolene decided to call his bluff.

"Well," I said after a long moment of silence, during which Jolene finished most of her coffee. "People make mistakes. I'm glad you told me the truth."

She stared. Her hand reached for the coffee cup but missed by several inches. The sedative was kicking in. It probably made it even harder for her to process my reaction. She finally grasped the cup and finished drinking the coffee, spilling just a little down her chin. Probably hoping the caffeine would clear the fog in her brain.

"What about Jack?" she asked, her words a little slurred.

"He already told me," I lied. "We had a long talk, and we made a deal for future situations. He won't do this kind of shit without running it by me first and vice versa."

"So..." she licked her lips, "you're forgiving him?"

I shrugged. "He's not my husband. I have no claims on him or his dick. We've been in a bit of a rough patch lately. It wasn't clear if we were together or not most days. He's sorry for going behind my back, so yeah, I forgive him. It's not like he broke some kind of oath. He just got bored. I get bored sometimes too."

I didn't forgive him. Not by a long shot. Her utter disappointment in my reaction made it worth looking like an idiot for these few moments. Melanie might just be a genius for suggesting the high road.

"Okay." She stood but had to grip the edge of the table to steady herself. "I don't feel so great."

"I know."

"Pardon?"

Instead of explaining, as tiresome villains in bad fiction tend to do, I waited. It took about three full minutes (I counted) for her to sink to the floor and pass out. I pushed the table away and then got the extension cord from the cabinet next to the window. True, I could've been more aggressive, just clobbered her over the head or shot her, but I'm Canadian, and that's not the way we operate. I also hate cleaning. Bludgeoning a person meant blood. Less mess was best.

I wrapped the cord around her neck, wound the ends around my hands a few times, and then I pulled with all my might. She opened her eyes near the end. I was glad. More satisfying to know she knew what was happening. She'd understand before she went into The Great Beyond that she picked the wrong home to wreck.

Now, I'll admit strangling was a poor choice on my part, less mess or not. It's personal. Intimate. Definitely more intimate than I wanted to be with Jolene. It also takes a long time, and it's not really clear when you're done. I paused once, because I thought she'd stopped breathing, but then she took a giant gulp of air and I had to resume pulling the cord. It dug into her neck, breaking the skin, and making the process a little slipperier than I anticipated, but I'm going to be honest here; the slick warmth of that blood on my hands sent a little thrill over my skin.

When they describe a killer getting sexual satisfaction out of killing, it's not entirely accurate. Yes, there's a level of arousal, but it's deeper than you'd experience with mere sex. It's more primal. There's a euphoric buzzing that begins in the tips of your fingers and spreads over your body until it weaves itself into your soul. And you don't orgasm as you would when you've reached the peak during intercourse. In fact, there is no definitive moment of release. It's like a slow, constant quiver in your nethers. The feeling gradually dissipates, but it can be called back if you focus hard enough, and it'll wash over you again almost as intensely as it does during the act itself. When it fades, though, you're left with a breath-sucking void in your soul, and you know the only way to fill it, to feel on top of the world once more, is to kill again.

I promised myself, as I knelt over my first official victim while she drew her last breaths, that I wouldn't fall into that trap. I'd enjoy this feeling, but when it leaves me, I won't kill just to get the feeling back. No one will die by my hand who doesn't deserve killing.

I twisted the cord around my fist one more time and pulled as hard as I could. Finally, the spark of life left her eyes and she let out a last poof of air and a fart. I held the cord tight for ninety seconds after that, so I wouldn't be fooled again, and then released it to stand. I picked up my phone, sent a text to Jolene that read, "Hey, I'm running late. Flat tire. Reschedule for tomorrow?" and then turned back to the dead body on my floor.

Since it was my first intentional homicide, and I improvised, which caused unforeseen issues, covering my tracks took some time. First, I had to decide if she stayed in one piece or many. My serial killer obsession actually made me pretty knowledgeable about what works and what doesn't when getting rid of a body. I also knew dismemberment was messy and always left evidence behind. I chose it anyway, because I didn't want to make it easy for the cops to put the pieces together, metaphorically or literally.

As long as I didn't give the cops reason to search my house, it wouldn't matter if bits of Jolene got missed. I didn't plan to give them reason.

I gathered some tools Jack left in my garage and a roll of plastic that was supposed to go over the basement windows last winter. He'd never know I used them, of course, because that'd be a piece of info that led back to me. If someone found them at his house and some DNA I missed got him a murder charge... Well, never leave your shit at your girlfriend's house, boys, especially if you think you might betray her by fucking a whackado. She might not break things off or kill you, but she could implicate you in a homicide.

I spread the plastic over the floor and up the walls in my basement. After removing her clothes, which I'd have to wear so the neighbors saw "her" leaving, I dragged her naked body downstairs. I was going to do it in the bathtub initially but trying to haul her into the tub was bullshit. You think you're strong until you try to lift a dead body. I half-lifted, half-rolled her into the plastic covered basement and decided to do it right there. The entire process left me with a pulled muscle in my neck and a bruise on my hip.

The first cut was the hardest because I had to get past the ick factor before I could truly get down to business. Once I did, it was smooth sailing. I put each of her pieces in a separate bag. Then I put the bag of garbage bags, which I paid cash for, into the bag containing her head. I knew they had ways of using those bags to find killers. No way were they staying in my house.

It was almost midnight by the time I carried the bags to the car. The neighbors might not see "her" leave. Hell, I don't even know if they noticed her at all. The only potential kink in my plan, I guess. I chose not to think about it as I drove out of town. The rest of the night was spent discarding her pieces several kilometers apart, in dumpsters, shallow holes, and deep lakes. Identifying pieces, like her head, had to be disposed of so they'd never be found. There's a quarry outside of town. It was very deep, very wide, and almost impossible to access without killing yourself. I tossed the bag containing her head and many heavy rocks into it and waited for it to sink before driving away.

The car was more difficult to dispose of. I knew there was no way to avoid someone stumbling across it, so I parked it at her apartment building. Her purse went into the fire pit in my backyard, but not until I took her phone out to send myself a few angry texts, because even if the phone is gone, law enforcement has ways of triangulating signals and retrieving text messages.

"I waited at Tim Horton's for two hours. WHERE

ARE YOU?" I texted myself from her phone, but then decided it looked like we'd had a fight, which could potentially point fingers my way. So, I added another message from Jolene that read, "Are you okay? Just saw your text. Did you get home? Where are you? I can pick you up."

Then I sent a text to Jack asking if he'd heard from me. Jack, bless his heart, replied, "I told u not to text me." I replied, as Jacqueline, "We were meeting for coffee. She got a flat tire, and I haven't heard anything since." Jack replied immediately, "Haven't heard from her. Stop texting me."

Poor Jack. I shook my head as I texted myself again, "Jack hasn't heard from you either. Please call me." Satisfied with my forensic countermeasures, I tossed her keys in a public trash can on my way home. I didn't call it a night right away. Instead, I drove a few miles outside of town and pulled over. I jabbed a knife from work into the bottom of a tire and waited while the air whistled out excruciatingly slowly. Someone stopped to help me after about an hour. I knew him, sort of. He came into the store all the time. I told him I'd been standing there for hours. My phone died, so I couldn't call for help.

He helped me change the tire and I was on my way home to clean up the mess I made while dismembering Jolene. Jack called several times, but I didn't answer, because my phone was supposed to be dead. Finally, after I was sure all traces of Jolene were gone, I texted Jolene and Jack the same message. "Sorry. Phone died. Just got home. See you tomorrow?"

He replied right away. "U Ok? Y didn't u call me?"

I sighed. "PHONE. DIED." I texted. "I'm fine."

"Ok. Day off?"

"Yes. Feeling like shit. See you tomorrow?"

"Sure. Love u."

"Love you too." I hated how he texted. Just type the whole word. What's it take, like a second more to spell it out? God.

Anyone with half a brain will notice the holes in my plan. I noticed them as well. The important thing here was not that Jolene would be found, but that my involvement was impossible to see. I think I succeeded. Time would tell.

Would I do it again?

Yes. Definitely.

The Swindler

If you work long enough in retail, you see all kinds. The Karens, the cheapskates, the thieves, the dirtbags, and the swindlers. Beth was a good con artist. She was smart. Also fucking batshit, but she was smart enough that the batshit factor didn't seem to work against her as it might others. Not for a while anyway. Eventually, crazy catches up with you, though.

She'd been coming in every Saturday for a couple of months, demanding a senior's discount. We don't do that at our store. Never have. Beth, though, would not be deterred. She wanted that discount, even if it only amounted to a couple of bucks saved here and there.

I rarely worked Saturday mornings, but I agreed to cover for Melanie one week, and I got the privilege of dealing with Beth one-on-one. Up to this point, I'd only seen her in passing and heard stories about her from my coworkers.

She'd moved into the house across the road from the store. Set up cameras all over the place, recording her neighbors, our parking lot, and the store next to her. She also recorded the street behind and to the left of her house. What she hoped to catch on those cameras, I don't know. Maybe she just had so many enemies from her conning bullshit that she had to sleep with one eye open. It's really anyone's guess. A few locals claimed she didn't have to work anymore; thanks to lawsuits she'd won against other businesses. If we parked on the street next to her house, she'd run out and make chalk marks next to our tires, and then call the by-law officer to claim we'd violated some kind of rule. If no one came by to issue a ticket, she'd march into the store and demand we move the vehicle. She recorded every interaction on her phone too. We knew this thanks to emails she'd sent to Corporate with the recordings attached.

Corporate wanted us to start offering seniors' discounts to shut her up. Other stores in the chain did it, apparently, but Bill was a little annoyed because they'd never made him aware of this policy. He resisted at first, but not for long. The day before my encounter with Beth, he announced we would start offering seniors' discounts. I should mention that staff got fuck all. No discount. No deals. Nada. Zip. But hey, if you're a crazy person who hurls abuse enough times at people who have done nothing wrong, you get a discount.

Corporate was supposed to have programmed the registers so we could do this beginning Saturday. They sent us instructions on how to remove ten percent from the bill when someone asked for the discount. The customer, who was claiming to be over sixty-five in order to get the discount, had to show identification to prove their age.

And now we come back to Beth. I didn't realize she was in the store that day until Leah paged me to cash. I approached, saw Beth, and groaned. Well, at least she'd get her fucking discount, right? I shouldn't be yelled at, threatened or abused. It should be a pleasant transaction with no hiccups.

Wrong.

"Button's not working," Leah said. "I can't give the discount."

I picked up the instruction sheet Corporate had provided with their email and went through the steps. Leah was right. It wouldn't work.

"She wouldn't show me identification either," Leah said in a low voice. "I just want her out of here, so I was going to give her the discount without it."

"What's going on?" Beth asked. "Corporate said I'd get a discount."

"I know," I said, trying to sound polite. "And I'm sorry, but the button isn't working."

"So?"

"So that means I have no way to discount your bill."

"Just take the tax off."

I sighed. Yeah, and you'll report me, and I'll be fined and fired. No thanks. "Sorry, but I can't do that either. It's kind of illegal. If you come back when the button is fixed, we can give you the discount. Right now, there's nothing I can do. The computers won't allow us to adjust the prices."

"I want my money."

"I can't just give you the money." I could, technically, and just short the register, but fuck her. Besides, she'd have the receipt, which doesn't show she received the discount, and she'd probably say she didn't get shit, and I'd still be in trouble.

I had little time to change my mind on the matter because Beth lost her shit. She demanded an apology. Said we were unprofessional. I pointed out that I did apologize. Twice. She got angrier. Leah confirmed I apologized.

"Don't be smart, you little bitch," Beth growled at Leah. "And don't tell me what I heard."

"I'm telling you what I said," I told her. "Maybe you didn't hear me. Maybe you did. The point is I can't give you a discount today. Believe me, I wish I could." I didn't wish that at all. I just wanted her to fuck off.

She did not fuck off. Instead, she started screaming. Her transaction was done. She'd paid. Bags were in her cart. Nothing more to do but leave. She kept screaming at Leah and me. Called us unprofessional again. Mentioned discrimination. Threatened to sue. Called Leah a little bitch again. Put her finger in my face, so close I could bite it off, and told me I was a stupid cunt.

I felt the familiar warmth of embarrassment wash over my skin as her words blended into a persistent but unintelligible buzz. How many times had I stood in this position, smile planted firmly on my face, while someone spoke to me like I was less than human? How many times had I swallowed their insults, even apologized for "making" them say such things, while quietly simmering inside? How many times had numerous strangers watched the exchange and not a single one tried to step in and help a girl out?

Beth spat on the debit machine and, finally, I reached my limit for her shenanigans.

"You can leave now," I said.

"Oh, can I?"

"Yes, I'm not arguing with you. People are waiting to pay for their groceries, so I'm sorry we can't give you the discount this time. I'll make sure it's fixed before your next visit. Have a nice weekend."

She looked like she might argue more but took her cart full of groceries and left. I watched as she walked across the road, wishing she'd drop dead of a heart attack. She didn't.

The next afternoon, I got reamed by my boss for not being polite enough. I corrected him, of course. I couldn't have been *more* polite if you ask me. Fuck, I never told her to suck a dick or anything I wanted to tell her. I *apologized*, for crying out loud. Twice. I didn't have to do that.

"She wants an apology," he said.

"Better not hold her breath," I replied.

"It's a formality. She got her discount this morning. Now, we just make nice."

"Guess you'll have to fire me," I said. Honestly, if he fired me, he'd have been next on my list. "Because I am not apologizing to that woman."

"Don't be dramatic."

"Don't *you* be dramatic," I countered. "I was nice. I was polite. I apologized for *your* boss' fuck up and I told her to have a nice weekend. She called Leah a stupid bitch and she called me a cunt. A *cunt,* Bill."

"Okay, but—"

"*And* then," I said, not letting him get a word in, "she spat on the debit machine. So, no, there'll be no apologies or politeness. In fact, you both can kiss my ass."

He sighed. "Look, Corporate just wants her to go away. We've gotta deal with her every week, so if she comes in again and you get her, just don't be rude. If she demands an apology, do your best to make her happy."

"I won't kill her. How's that?"

"And don't tell me to kiss your ass. It sets a bad example."

"It was a general statement."

"Promise you won't be rude to her."

"When have I ever?"

Bill raised his eyebrow but said no more. He returned to his computer, loaded another game of solitaire, and I returned to work.

I waited another week to see Beth again. She walked in, righteous as fuck, and filled a cart. At checkout, she asked for the seniors' discount. The cashier asked for identification. She lost her shit. Sadly, my boss was in that day, so I didn't get a chance to "make nice." When a manager was paged, he came downstairs. After more yelling about discrimination from Beth, he told the cashier to give her the discount without the identification.

Pussy.

I watched the whole scene, arms folded over my chest, and rolled a few ideas around in my head. I could break into her house, but the fucking cameras...maybe she could have an accident in the store. It'd be hard, what with the accidents I'd already been a part of.

With Beth, I'd have to be creative. Smarter. I stood there watching her leave, hating my boss for his lack of balls, and seethed. She probably wasn't even sixty-five. Sure, she looked rough, but I'd put her in her fifties at most. Lying piece of shit.

As she reached the lights at the intersection, she

crossed on a flashing yellow. About halfway across, she turned back to look at the store and waved. Her big shit-eating grin annoyed me to my core. The light was now red. To the right, a transport rumbled its way toward her. Smiling, I walked to the window, where I knew she could see me, and lifted my middle finger.

She was so caught up in her indignation at my little act of defiance, she didn't see the transport coming until it sent her flying through the air. Her groceries went with her. Cans rolled toward the gutter, while a few oranges splatted on the ground next to the now stopped transport. Beth landed in the crosswalk on the opposite side of the road, arms and legs bent at awkward angles.

People rushed toward her. The driver of the truck got out, pale as a ghost, and lifted his phone to his ear. Poor fucker. Wasn't his fault. She crossed on a red light. It was too late for him to stop.

While I was a little disappointed that I didn't get to take care of Beth, I thanked the universe for saving me the trouble of coming up with a plan. Gratitude, I imagine, is important to the cosmic forces at work here. I'd never do anything that might anger those forces.

Everyone stood at the windows or rushed outside to watch the shit show. I returned to Receiving and kept working, humming a happy tune as I did so.

The Rapist

The most annoying thing about rapists, aside from the raping, is their punishment never fits their crime. Drug possession, illegal use of a firearm (shooting squirrels in your backyard with a gun you forgot to register, for example), and theft often carry harsher sentences. When it comes to rape, the victim has to prove it happened, so it's not a matter of showing the damage caused or matching the DNA like they do on television. In real life, you have to prove *you* didn't *want* to be fucked. You have to prove you don't like it rough or didn't lead him on.

As you may have guessed, the next degenerate in this story is a rapist who liked young girls, although he didn't discriminate against older women. We're all fair game to this guy.

Derek was an attractive man. In fact, when I was younger, I had a major crush on him. His smile could charm the panties off a nun, and he had a personality to match. Women loved him, is what I'm saying. He didn't have to work hard to get into someone's pants. Plenty of women wanted to fuck him and did. Too bad he wanted the ones who said no more than he wanted the ones who'd hop in his bed willingly.

While he got caught, and was charged with

several assaults, just one charge stuck. Only one victim out of at least a half dozen managed to convince a judge she didn't want him to fuck her, and then a few of the other charges slipped away in a plea deal. They also managed to get him on statutory rape, but his sentence was less than the time he already spent in jail awaiting trial, so...yeah. Anyway, he did a few months and was out. The town embraced him, and all sins were forgiven.

I watched him come into the store, talk with the young girls on cash, flirt and joke around, and be totally accepted, despite being a disgusting waste of flesh. It infuriated me. People who knew better practically kissed his sorry ass. It was like they just forgot what a degenerate he was. In this town, though, if you don't talk about it, then maybe it never happened.

"Hey," he'd say as he came through my register. "How are you?"

The way he said it was friendly enough, but I felt like his eyes were boring through my clothes. I'm not arrogant enough to believe I'm irresistible to men. I've got my flaws. Many of them. However, knowing what I knew about Derek, the simple fact that I didn't like him probably made me a target. It wasn't about sex or being attractive. He wasn't horny or hot for my body. It was about power. It's always about power, ladies. Don't let those fuckers making you feel bad about your short skirt or that extra cocktail tell you otherwise. You could have warts, cellulite, greasy hair, razor burn on your chin, and wear a hazmat suit when you go out on the town, and they'd *still* come after you.

Derek liked to be in charge. He had to prove something to these ungrateful bitches who dared to claim they didn't want him. Knowing that if I said no, he'd just carry on anyway made me feel uncomfortable. I don't like feeling vulnerable like that.

One evening, as he eyed Ava, a new hire barely into high school, I realized I could use his need to dominate as a weapon. I mean, I don't look like much. Guys like him wouldn't think I could fight back. That gave me the upper hand.

I walked to Ava's register, told her to go face shelves, and finished ringing the customer ahead of Derek through. He glared at me. I knew that he knew I sent Ava away because of him. He put his stuff on the belt without a word, eyed me as I scanned it through.

"Bags?" I asked.

"Yes."

I put his groceries into bags and then pressed "total." "That's twenty-three-fifty-two."

He held up a debit card. I pressed the appropriate button and waited for him to do his thing.

"You still over on River?" he asked.

"Yep."

"Heard the cop moved out."

A cop used to live across the street. He moved last summer. "He did. A retired couple moved in. They're nice."

He nodded as the machine beeped, approving his card. "I sense that you don't like me."

"Why would you think that?" I asked and forced a smile.

"Just...something. You know I didn't do what they said."

"You didn't fuck a kid?"

"That was a misunderstanding. She was seventeen. Hardly a kid."

"If you say so."

"I meant the rape. She was lying."

"Yet you plead guilty."

"I only did that to save my family from the stress of a trial."

"Is that so? What about the other women? How many were there? Five? Six?"

No one was behind him, so I was forced to stay and talk. It killed me not to smash his face off the belt or shove the scanner gun down his throat.

"Eleven, but they lied."

Oh, *more* than a half dozen. Jesus Christ. "Eleven women, who didn't know each other, from different towns... They all lied?"

"I'm not saying I never slept with them. I did, but I wasn't interested in a relationship with any of them, so they were bitter."

"All of them?"

"Yes, all of them. I mean, no one likes to be rejected. What I'm saying is they saw a chance to get some revenge when I got arrested, and wanted a little attention, so they jumped on the bandwagon. My lawyer said it's like mob mentality took over. Happens all the time. Guys sleep around and women get angry and cry rape. It's really a problem for the justice system."

"No, I don't think the women are the problem."

"I'm just saying, if that's why you don't like me, you should know the truth."

"I know the truth," I said.

"Okay." He picked up his bags. "I'll see you around."

"Sure."

I watched him leave. As the doors closed behind him, I shuddered. I'd have to shower with bleach to wash the creep off me. That exchange solidified my decision to get rid of him. It didn't take long to figure out how to do it either.

My plan was to somehow lure him into a situation where we were alone. Once I had him, I'd self-defense my way into killing him. I knew I could do it and I'd get away with it, but the goddamn virus arrived, and shit got weird.

I suppose I should cover that first.

The Plague

When you think you've finally become good at what you do, be it killing assholes or selling potatoes and whatnot, and you've gotten all your ducks in a row, the universe has to throw a wrench into your plans. That's what the universe does, I think. It seeks out perfection and says, "I must fuck that shit up."

I don't read the news much. I mean, aside from major stories about events that might affect me, I ignore much of what I see in the headlines. Because of this willful ignorance, I was not prepared for the weekend that the virus made shit go sideways.

I came in at three o'clock that Thursday in March. Derek always came in at closing, and I had my attack all planned out. It was going to be perfect.

Thursday's closing shift is usually uneventful, so imagine my surprise when I saw the full parking lot as I approached the building. Then, I went inside, and my coworkers looked like they'd been to war. Hair askew, faces flushed, clothes dirty and disheveled, and that haunted stare we see in photos from combat zones.

"What's up?" I asked. "It's not check day, is it?"

Leah looked at me with a bit of a What the fuck? expression. "Have you been on Facebook or anything?"

I mean, I had been on Facebook, but only to play

Candy Crush, so I shook my head. "No, why?"

That's when Melanie came through the doors to the receiving area. "We're out of toilet paper, hand sanitizer, all the cleaners, bananas, yeast, and milk."

I stared. It was an odd combination of items to run out of.

"Fuck me," Leah groaned.

"What's going on?" I asked.

Melanie gave me the same look Leah had and then rubbed her face with the palm of her hand. "They're talking about quarantines and closing borders, so everyone's going fucking batshit. Buying everything in the damn store. I had to hide the baby wipes so people with actual babies would have some."

"Oh." I nodded. It was a lot to unpack. I focused on what seemed like the most important detail in her speech. "And why are we talking about quarantines?"

"That Corona virus is in Canada," Leah explained. "It's been killing people in China, like hardcore. Have you seriously not watched the news?"

"I mean, not today."

"They've been talking about China for months."

"Really?" I was dumbfounded. To be honest, I recalled reading something about it, but I thought it'd be like every other virus that the media made a stink about: it'd be bad for a bit, but it'd go away and not really affect us. After all, initial reports said it was only deadly for old or immunocompromised people. Kids were immune and healthy people were just going to catch an annoying cold. How bad could that possibly be?

I've never been so wrong about a thing in my life.

"I hope you're ready for a shit show," Melanie said. "They're fucking nuts."

The few hours between Melanie leaving and closing were hectic. People loaded carts to overflowing. They yelled at cashiers. They demanded toilet paper we didn't have. Accused us of hoarding a stash in the back room.

"I insist you go look," one woman said to me. "I know you have more."

"Do you?" I said as I unloaded a case of dog treats.

"Well? Are you going to look or not?"

"Nope."

"You have to."

I set the empty box down and looked at her. You see, I was past giving a shit about my job at this point. "We ran out of toilet paper before noon. There is no more. Staff didn't get any, because we had two skids of it and didn't think we'd run out. No one who works here is hoarding a damn thing. It's all gone. So, no, I'm not going to look, because I don't have to. It's not there."

"I'll be calling head office about your attitude."

"Have at it," I said and resumed stocking the shelf.

In the hour that followed, we also ran out of paper towel, tissues, and canned mushrooms. By the time I said goodbye to the cashiers and locked the door, we had also run out of sugar, ground beef, and cereal. Derek didn't come in, but I no longer cared about killing him. I was exhausted and I wanted to kill everyone.

As I counted the registers, a loud pounding on the window scared the bejesus out of me. I turned. A tall, burly man with a beard and a dirty trucker's cap stood there. He pointed to the door. I shook my head and said, "We're closed."

"Fucking bitch," he screamed. "Open the door."

He clearly didn't know who he was messing with.

"Closed," I said dramatically, just in case he couldn't hear me.

"Fuck you," he screamed again, punching the window. It shuddered, but thankfully, didn't break. "Miserable cunt!"

One more swipe at the window and he got into his truck. He didn't leave, though.

I continued with closing, checked the back doors to make sure everything was locked up, and looked outside. Still in his truck. Motherfucker.

All I wanted to do was go home, put my feet up,

and Google this Corona shit to see how bad this situation really was. Instead, I was forced to wait out this fuck-nut. I sat on the stairs that led up to the offices, where I could see the edge of his truck, but he couldn't see me.

"Who's the killer here?" I asked myself. We might both be killers, to be honest, but I had a good feeling this fucknut couldn't kill a fly without getting caught. I took a breath, grabbed my bags, and left the store.

He didn't get out but revved the engine while I locked up. I pretended not to notice. He obviously didn't have the balls to do more, or I'd have two hundred pounds of redneck on my back. Coward.

That was the tip of the iceberg, kids. In the weeks that followed, I was spat on, shoved, threatened with all kinds of physical violence, called a bitch, a whore, an asshole, and every other nasty word you can think of. A couple of people even told me to die. Nice, right?

I was proud of myself for not giving into the urge to fuck a bitch up. I stayed calm. I stayed professional. They weren't going to steer me away from my purpose. Average assholes didn't get to die. They might deserve it, but they weren't going to badger me into doing something stupid. Besides, the Corona would take care of most of them in the end. I had faith in the universe to work that shit out without me.

And then two potential targets arrived at the

same time. The first was Adam. I didn't know his name until much later. He was a ginger, and his friend was a tall Asian fellow. Their other friend, who I didn't see, entered the store ahead of them, while Adam went to the Beer Store next door. He came out later, tried to walk right in, but our door guy Bob (security guard of sorts) stopped him.

"Sorry, pal," Bob said. "You gotta get in line with everyone else."

"My friend is inside. We're just meeting up with him."

"Still gotta get in line. It's one person at a time."

We were only allowed to let so many people in the store. This ensured everyone could stay six feet away from others. They also had to wear a mask and take a cart. Everyone had a problem with at least one of these rules. Just a little background so you all understand where we're at in terms of lunacy. Anyway, Adam walked to the end of the line with his buddy, got his phone out, turned on the camera, and then waited. When it was their turn, Bob asked them if they were shopping or were they just joining their buddy inside. As part of our limiting the number of people in the store, we discouraged anyone not actually buying something from going inside. Made the lineup a little shorter. Not everyone liked to be discouraged. Adam, apparently, was counting on this.

As he reached the front of the line, he held his phone in Bob's face. Bob, bless him, didn't question the phone. "Are you experiencing fever, shortness of breath or a dry cough?" he asked.

"No," Adam said.

"Body aches, chest tightness, headache, nasal congestion, or stomach irritation like nausea or diarrhea?"

"No."

"And are you two going in to shop or are you just meeting your friend inside?"

"Why? Do you have a problem with Asians?"

Bob shook his head. "Are you shopping or not, man?"

"You're a racist."

"I'm not racist, buddy," Bob said. "Just asking a question. I need to know if you guys are buying or just tagging along. We can only let so many people in at a time, so if you're not buying, you don't need to go in."

Adam continued to scream at the top of his lungs about racists, holding his phone up the whole time. Bob waved at the cashiers inside, which was our sign that they needed to call a manager to the door.

I arrived as Adam tried to push past Bob. Bob didn't let him past but didn't push him out either. He and his pal, who said nothing, stood their ground, as though trying to intimidate Bob. Bless their hearts too.

Why not, right?

"What's up?" I asked, mentally preparing for the abuse to start.

Adam turned his angry scowl on me. "Why is the Asian forced to stand outside while all the white people are allowed to go inside?"

"Well," I said, glancing at Bob who shook his head, "it might be because the Asian's friend is out here screaming like a lunatic."

"You think this is a Chinese virus, but it isn't. He's not even Chinese. It's racist to even assume that you know anything about it."

I sighed. "I never said it was a Chinese virus. Never said anything about China because race has nothing to do with this situation. We just don't let crazy people inside."

"I'm recording this!"

"Okay," I said. "That's fine. Whatever floats your boat."

"Why is the Asian forced to stay outside?" he asked again. "You're letting all the white people in."

It was going to be like this. "I told you already, it's got nothing to do with race. You're screaming and he's with you. If you calm down, you both can go in."

"He said I'd lose." He pointed at Bob. "What does that mean? Why will I lose? Because my friend is Asian?"

I raised an eyebrow at Bob.

"He tried to push me," Bob explained. "I got a little heated and told him if he got aggressive, he'd lose."

"Yeah," Adam screamed, phone in my face. "I'll lose because my friend is Asian. You're racist."

Fuck, right? I saw this was going to a bad place the second he said "racist." It was already at a bad place, but it was quickly traveling to "worse," so I turned to Adam, placing myself between him and Bob, and put my hand in front of his phone, which was recording my chest at this point. "Look, I think you misunderstood what he was saying, and I—"

"He knows English!" Adam screamed. "How dare you assume that the Asian guy doesn't know English."

"I'm talking to *you*, not your friend, and it's clear you understand English. What I'm saying is *you* got upset before Bob could explain himself."

Bob waved two women inside from behind me. They quickly grabbed their carts and scurried past Adam and his friend.

"Why are all the white people going in?" Adam screamed. "No one's stopping *them!*"

"If you calm down, you can go in too. I have no problem with you or your friend. Bob doesn't have a problem either."

"Then why are we standing out here?"

"You're acting like a crazy person. That's why. Those people are answering Bob's questions and they're not yelling at him. If you stop making threats and accusations, you can go in. Are you going to calm down?"

Adam, sails deflated, lowered his phone. "I want the owner's name and number, and I want his name," he pointed at Bob, "and your name. I want to know who to report this blatant racism to."

I sighed. "Okay. I'll get all of that for you. Just calm down and you can do your shopping."

Adam walked to the interior door but turned before entering the store. "Who is the loser, huh?" He gave Bob the finger. "I win, asshole. I win!"

"Enough!" I yelled loud enough to make Adam take a few steps back. "Shut your fucking mouth or leave." Bob started to say something, but I pointed at him. "You're going to shut your fucking mouth or you're leaving too. This has gone far enough. No more."

"I want your name too," Adam said, although he lowered his voice. "Can't speak to me like that."

"Whatever, buddy. Just do your shopping and get the fuck out of here."

He went inside, slowly. His Asian friend, maybe realizing Adam was bananas, returned to their car. The door closed and I got the whole story of what led up to the shit show from Bob and customers waiting outside.

Basically, Adam, the asshole, set the whole thing up from the start. He was recording the people in line with him, as well as Bob, and whispering to his friend. One customer claimed to have heard him say, "I'll do all the talking," to the friend as they approached the door. So, he wanted us to say something offensive. He purposely provoked Bob who, thankfully, didn't take the bait.

When Adam got to cash register, I could see that he and his friend bought nothing. They exited, I handed Adam a scrap of paper with the information he requested on it, but Adam wasn't done. Phone raised, still recording, he started screaming again. Same stuff. Same questions. Over and over again. Finally, I sent Bob inside and then turned to face Adam.

"Look, you're not getting what you want," I said. "Bob answered your questions. You think he's lying, but he insists he's not. No one is going to be happy today. That's the end of it. File a complaint if you want but get out of here. I'm done with your bullshit."

Adam walked close enough for our chests to touch. "You're a racist bitch."

"Sure. If believing that makes you happy, I'm a racist bitch. I'll probably go straight to hell. Now fuck off."

"I'll have your job. I recorded everything."

"Good. I'm not really enjoying it at the moment."

He bumped me with his chest. It wasn't a hard

shove. Just enough to let me know he could do worse. That was my breaking point. I'd made it five long months without losing my cool. Then this fucker comes in and accuses me of being the worst kind of human being before trying to physically intimidate me into making a poorly thought-out comment in return? I don't think so.

"You've got three seconds to back the fuck off and leave," I said calmly.

"Or what?"

You'll see, asshole.

"Three...two..."

He flipped his middle finger at me and then walked away. I watched him and his friend walk to their car, wrote down the license plate number, and then went back to work.

My mind worked furiously to figure out a way to make Adam pay when the second problem appeared. Her name was Nancy. She was an overweight woman in her mid-forties, although the lines on her face made her look much older.

Now, not everyone had to wear masks at this point in the pandemic. If they claimed a medical exemption, we let them in the store. One person per household, take a cart, sanitize your hands, wear gloves. Those were the rules we would not bend. Nancy came in, ditched her cart in aisle one, and proceeded, gloveless, maskless, while hacking and coughing, to aisle two, where she picked up Tylenol, Buckley's, and several packages of throat lozenges.

The other very important rule of going out and about during a pandemic was that you NEVER went anywhere if you had a single symptom of Covid. Watching Nancy, I counted at least three. Snot, cough, and shortness of breath. Probably had a fever, but we weren't allowed to check for that. Civil rights bullshit.

Anyway, I slowly made my way to the registers. My plan was to follow Nancy out, take down her license plate, and report her to Public Health, so that if she were Covid positive, we could stop her from making someone else sick.

Well, Nancy had other ideas, I guess.

She tossed her medicine on Penny's belt and made her way to the end of the lane. Penny, bless her heart, worked tirelessly in the early days of Covid to keep herself and everyone around her safe. She did it all with a smile too, until Nancy.

"Are you sick?" Penny asked, her voice, already high-pitched, increasing a few decibels with each word.

"None of your business," Nancy said and then coughed. No, she didn't cover her mouth.

"I'm sorry, but you'll have to leave. You aren't allowed to be in the store with symptoms."

"Fuck you," Nancy replied. "Just ring my shit

through and stop being a whiny, sheep-ass bitch."

I walked closer, but not too close. I did not want what Nancy had, after all.

Penny opened her mouth, closed it, and then picked up the phone. "Bill to Cash One," she said over the loudspeaker. "Bill, Cash One."

"What are you doing?" Nancy asked.

"I'm paging the owner."

"What for?"

"To escort you out of the store."

"I'm not leaving."

And Bill wasn't coming. I realized after another exchange of insults from Penny and Nancy that Bill, ball-less fuck that he was, could see everything on the cameras upstairs and wasn't going to help. Sighing, I walked toward Penny's register. "Is there a problem?"

Penny pointed at Nancy. "She's got Covid symptoms and refuses to leave. I don't have to serve her. It's a matter of personal safety, so you can't make me."

"No, I can't. Ma'am, you're clearly sick. You should have someone pick up what you need or call for curbside. You can't be in here if you're sick."

"You can't refuse service," Nancy said. "I've got rights."

"So do I," Penny said. She was very pro-safety, particularly in her work environment. She wouldn't budge and she wasn't wrong. Nancy had had at least four coughing fits since I noticed her in the store, and she looked like she might collapse any second as she wheezed her way through her *fuck you*s and *suck a dick*s.

"I'm sorry, ma'am," I said. "Penny's right. You're violating a public health order by coming in with symptoms. If you don't leave, I'll have to call the police."

She stared at me for a second, and then turned to Penny. "You stupid little cunt," she said. "I'll have your fucking job."

Penny smiled. "Try it. I can't get fired for protecting myself and my customers. Now leave."

Nancy smirked and then did something that before Covid would've been just a nasty, asshole thing to do. Since Covid, it was akin to assault. She leaned forward, made a godawful hacking sound in her throat and spat in Penny's face.

I held my breath as the bright green loogie oozed down Penny's eyebrow, dripped over her cheek, and then pooled at her lips. She grabbed a paper towel and wiped her face, her hands shaking as she did so.

What a twat. I still can't believe she did it. In the moment, I only froze for a heartbeat, but quickly recovered. I took my cell phone from my pocket and dialed 9-1-1. Nancy turned to me.

"Don't even try it," I said as the operator picked up. "Because unlike Penny, I don't need this job and I'll knock you the fuck out. Leave. The cops are on their way."

Nancy seemed to consider spitting on me, but she didn't. She left, without her meds, and I followed her out as I told the operator I wanted to report an assault. My intention was to get Nancy's license plate number, but the bitch walked up the street and disappeared, so that was impossible. I wasn't sure where she lived either, so all I could tell the police, when they arrived two hours later, was that her name was Nancy and she lived in town.

They did nothing. If we'd had a plate number or an address, Penny could press charges. Since we had neither, nor did we have cameras that recorded, there was nothing we could do, for now. Penny left work immediately because she had to get tested for Covid and isolate.

Bill argued about whether or not she'd be paid. That man was practically begging to be killed.

So, my problems tripled that day. Who would it be? Not Bill. Not yet. I mean, who'd take over the store with him gone? Could be worse. The devil you know and all that. Besides, in the end, Corporate said he had to pay Penny, because she was exposed at work.

I didn't know where Nancy lived and we weren't

sure if she had Covid or not, so her spitting on Penny might have been harmless. Cruel and gross, sure, but harmless.

That left me with Adam. Nancy could wait. Adam had to be punished and, because he wasn't local, I only had so much time to see it done.

———

After closing, still pissed at Nancy and the dick-smack named Adam, I walked to the motel. I didn't find his car, so I walked further, out to the cottages at the edge of town. There, near the back of the property, I found them. I crept through the woods along the perimeter of the property until I found them seated in lawn chairs near the water. A fire crackled in the fire pit while the three of them laughed at something on Adam's phone. The video, probably.

"Can't sue with that," the Asian friend said. "They didn't bite. I told you I should've done the talking."

"Maybe," Adam said, scrolling through his phone. "Going to put it on YouTube anyway. That bitch will lose her job at least."

My face felt hot. The ends of my fingers and toes tingled. Fucking pricks. This couldn't stand. How many others had they done this to? How many people lost their jobs for it? Racist people deserve all the shit, but not innocent people just trying to get through the day.

I stared at the flames licking the edge of the rock-lined fire pit. The sun had just started setting. Soon, it'd be dark, and the almost empty campgrounds would be quiet. I noticed a gas can sitting near the porch of the cottage, about ten feet from the pit. Stupid tourists. That wasn't safe.

As an idea formed, I sank down to the damp ground and waited. No one saw me come in, and no one would notice me leave once the deed was done. I just had to wait.

They stayed outside until they finished the case of beer at their feet. Then they made a half-hearted attempt to douse the fire and staggered inside the cottage. Sitting on the wet ground for three hours isn't something I'd recommend. My knees ached and my pants were soaked and stained by the time the lights went out in the cottage. I made my way to the fire pit, crouching so I wouldn't be seen. A few embers still smoldered. One should always make sure the fire is totally out before walking away. They could burn the whole place down.

I crept to the porch, picked up the gas can, confirmed it was almost full, and then walked to the door. I looked around for something to block it with but found nothing. I picked up a piece of kindling, jammed it in the narrow space between the door handle and the porch railing, and then stepped back. It might stay, it might not. If the whole porch was ablaze, it'd be hard to leave. That'd do.

I poured the gasoline onto the old planks of the porch steps and then splashed some up the wooden screen door. Then I walked around the cottage, spilling gasoline along the ground beneath the windows. Once I was satisfied that I'd blocked all exits, I made a trail of gasoline all the way to the fire pit and then to the empty cottages nearby. It'd be hard to see Adam as a target if someone burned it all down, right? Sucks for the owners of the cottages, but their insurance would give them even better cottages that they could charge more for in the end. I was kind of doing them a favor.

I inhaled the acrid fumes while making sure no one was watching me. The only lights on were those that lit up the dock near the main building. Everyone else slept. I carefully poured the remaining gas into the fire pit. The embers flared to life again, and I tossed the can toward the porch before retreating to the shelter of trees where I'd hidden while listening to Adam and his friend.

The flames took a while to jump from the pit to the gas-soaked ground next to it. Once they did, though, it took little time for them to devour the old wood-framed cottage. I took off as soon as the fire licked at the windows. I didn't need to see the rest. Better to be far from the scene before anyone realized what was up.

By the time I arrived home I heard the sirens. I stayed up all night, waiting for someone to report it on Facebook. Finally, a night owl friend posted pictures of the carnage I left and confirmed what I'd hoped would happen. The occupants of the cottage that the fire chief believed to be the source of the blaze, didn't make it out. That was when I learned Adam's name. Not that it matters. Thought you might be curious, is all.

The fire burned the empty cottages behind Adam's and caused significant damage to the boats nearby. A prank gone wrong, they figured, but the investigation was still underway, so they didn't say much else.

I tossed my clothes in the washing machine before going to bed. As I drifted off to sleep, I wondered how long this pandemic nonsense would last. Would it force me to kill anyone else? It was kind of the perfect situation for me to do it without suspicion.

It wasn't until sleep almost claimed my brain that I thought about Derek and then Nancy. If Adam and his friend deserved death, how could I let Derek and Nancy get away with their crimes? The answer was simple: I couldn't.

Typhoid Nancy

So, it turned out Nancy was a regular customer. She came in the first week of every month, after receiving her government check, and a few times between if her supply of potato chips and cigarettes ran low and she had enough cash left to get more.

Penny had been off two days when we got a call from Public Health. A customer tested positive for Covid. They wouldn't name names, but we all knew who it was. Fucking Nancy.

I asked around, because it's not hard getting personal information in a small town, and found out where Nancy lived. Sadly, she didn't live alone. The shit hole she called home was a triplex and she had two people living in her unit with her. I couldn't get in unnoticed, and I'd never hurt someone who didn't deserve it.

But how else was I supposed to deal with her?

The answer presented itself when Sam, our deli clerk, mentioned she was glad Nancy was in quarantine and she didn't miss her visits to the deli. You see, Nancy often leaned her sweaty tits on the glass separating the deli meat from customer spit and germs, and breathed all over the scale, where we weighed meat before packaging it. She'd been spreading disease before she had a disease worthy of spreading.

Penny's husband called to tell us she was in the hospital. The doctors figured she'd make a full recovery, but they couldn't promise that, because no one knew shit about the virus at this point. She was on oxygen, and they were doing all they could for her.

Nancy really was a menace.

Sam explained that Nancy made them custom make her sandwiches. Normally, we make standard sandwiches that we package and put in a cooler for customers to buy. We're not a restaurant, so we don't make them to order. Bill, however, said to make Nancy's without tomatoes and to use mayo instead of the mustard-mayo blend we normally use. She complained enough, apparently, to make Bill break the rule he put in place.

I knew she wouldn't comply with the isolation order, because she didn't seem able to follow any rules, so while I waited for her to come into the store, I researched how I might get justice for Penny. Turns out that Tylenol she so desperately wanted was actually pretty dangerous in large quantities. I did the math as best I could, and then decided that I could take the bottle containing about twenty Tylenol 2's that Jack left in my bathroom and crush about…all of them, and that should do the trick. She wasn't likely to die, but she'd at least lose some liver function and suffer for the rest of her life. I was okay with that outcome.

So, all I had to do was wait.

I carried the small vial of crushed Tylenol in my pocket for two days before Nancy visited the store. Mack saw her come in and waved me over.

"She shouldn't be in here," Mack said. "Should we call the cops?"

"No," I said. "I'll just deal with her. They'll take forever to get here, and I don't need her spitting on anyone else."

"She should be charged."

I nodded. "We'll report her, but not until after she's gone."

"All right," Mack said. "But I'm not going anywhere near her."

I watched Mack walk away and then headed toward the deli. Carol, the girl working behind the counter, saw Nancy as I approached. I could tell by the slight hunch in her shoulders. "Hey," I said. "I'll get this one."

"You sure?"

"I've worked Deli before. I can make a sandwich."

"I know but, she's infected. She should be asked to leave."

"It's okay," I said, pulling on a pair of gloves. "We don't need her spitting on anyone. Better to just get her in and out as quickly as possible."

Carol stepped back and allowed me to move behind the counter.

"Why don't you go on break?" I suggested. It'd be hard to add the Tylenol to the sandwich with a witness.

"Okay," Carol said. "If you don't mind."

"Not at all," I smiled as Nancy approached the counter. "Can I help you?"

She coughed before replying. "I want a sandwich."

"The ones on the shelf aren't good enough?" I mean, I knew what she wanted, but who says I have to make it easy?

"I don't like mustard or tomato. Bill said you guys had to make mine."

"Sure," I said with a pleasant smile. "What do you want on it?"

"Turkey, mayo, and lettuce. Oh, and the white cheese, not the yellow."

"Got it." I moved toward the prep counter. "Why don't you finish your shopping and come back? I'll be a few minutes."

She looked suspicious but nodded and moved away. As soon as she was out of sight, I quickly assembled the sandwich. After spreading way too much mayo on both sides of the bread, I removed the vial of Tylenol and sprinkled it on both sides. No way would she not taste that, I thought as I mixed it into the mayo.

"Is it done yet?" Nancy asked, making me jump a

little.

"Oh, yeah," I said quickly covering the mayo with the meat and lettuce. "You want pickles?"

"Sure, thanks," she said. "Maybe I'll actually be able to taste those."

My unease slipped away. That's right. Covid took away the sense of taste and smell sometimes. Clearly, a cosmic force far more powerful than me was at work here. I quickly added pickles and wrapped the sandwich before slapping a label on it and handing it to Nancy.

"Have a great day," I said.

"Thanks." Nancy said and then coughed all over the glass covering the deli meat.

Fucking pig. I let her pay and leave the store before I called Public Health and reported her for violating the quarantine order. If the sandwich didn't kill her, at least she'd have a hefty fine to pay.

Now, I know poisoning is so cliché. If anyone catches on to what I did, they'll definitely be looking for a woman, because it's how we like to get the job done. Female killers are typically non-violent, according to the so-called experts, because we're often smaller in stature than a man and we don't have the same need to cause pain when we kill. I believe, however, that our methods of killing have nothing to do with being violent or non-violent. Women simply choose the most expedient method, and that means we choose the one that does the job and isn't likely to get us caught. Poisoning is a distance kill, which allows us to be far away from the victim at the time of their death. Makes it harder for the cops to draw a line connecting us to the crime. It's just smart.

About two weeks later, Nancy's roommate, or boyfriend, whatever he was, came into the store. His eyes were red and puffy, and Leah asked if he was okay. He shook his head.

"Nancy died yesterday," he said.

"Nancy?"

"Yeah, she, uh, used to come in here all the time. Loved your sandwiches."

I smiled as I busied myself with stacking bags at the next register. I mean, I didn't intend to kill her, but the world wouldn't suffer from her loss.

"Oh, that's terrible," Leah said. "Did she have Covid?"

He nodded. "She was feeling better, though. Came in and got a sandwich the day before she got sicker. Walked the whole way too."

"Uh, aren't you supposed to quarantine with Covid?" Leah asked. She glanced at me, but I kept my head down.

"That's a load of shit," he said. "If you're feeling all right, you're not contagious."

"I don't think that's how it works." She put his

items into bags and then looked up sharply. "Did you get tested?"

"Nah," he sniffed. "I'm fine. Nancy was fine too, but after she went out that day, she ate the sandwich and felt shitty. I said it might have been the sandwich, some rotten meat or whatever, but she said it was the Covid. Took some Tylenol and went to bed."

"Oh dear," Leah murmured.

"She got up a few times with cramps. Started sweating. I said we should go to the hospital, but she'd had a bad fever from the Covid before, so she just took a couple more Tylenol to get it down and went back to bed again."

I knew where this was going. Leah, if her worried frown was anything to go by, did as well.

"Then," he continued, "I guess she got up a few times and took more. I don't know. They said her liver swelled or something. She might have pulled through, they said, if not for the Covid. It complicated the Tylenol poisoning. Something about already compromising her organs?"

"Shit," Leah whispered.

He sniffed. "Man, I thought she was only tired, so I let her sleep all day and night. If I'd known..." He sniffed again. "By the time I realized she really wasn't right, it was too late. Couldn't do nothing for her. She just went downhill so fast."

"Sorry," Leah said, careful to keep a safe distance from him as he grabbed his bag. "I'll, um, pray for you."

He left and I couldn't hold the laughter back any longer.

Leah looked at me. "You think it's funny?"

"You'll pray for him?"

Her cheeks pinkened. "Well, what else was I supposed to say?"

I shook my head. "I don't know."

I'd pray for him too, and every other idiot who refused to take this pandemic seriously, but not until after I dealt with Derek. Every day that passed meant he might concoct a better plan for getting me than I had for getting him.

And to be honest, I didn't have a plan yet. Not even an idea. I had to focus. Nancy got what she deserved and now it was Derek's turn. He didn't deserve an easy death like Nancy got. Someone like him should go bloody.

The Rapist...Again

Derek made daily visits to the store once the lockdown was lifted, and people were allowed to go back to work. He made a point of saying hello to me every time he came in. I didn't even try to be polite. Ignoring him was perfect bait. He couldn't get enough of my indifference.

We made it to stage three of a multi-stage reopening plan before shit went south again. It took just a couple of months for the government to start talking about a second lockdown. Infection rates had dropped, but with schools opening, they (predictably) spiked again. The government made threats every time they reported on case rates, so I knew it wouldn't be long before we were back to being stuck in our homes unless we were essential employees going to or from work. So did Derek. That meant if he was going to make his move, it had to be soon. I was ready.

He didn't disappoint.

The day Ontario's premier held a press conference that basically said a second lockdown was imminent, Derek showed up after closing. I had just sent everyone home, so I really shouldn't have let him into the store. That's like a golden rule; no employee is ever alone in the store with a customer. Our cameras don't record, so no one would know what happened if said customer robbed the place. If he killed me or I killed him, the truth of what took place would remain with us.

I planned to be the one walking out that night.

Before going to the door, I opened the drawer beneath Lane Two and removed the knife I stole from the meat department and stashed there when the pandemic started. Hey, you never know what people will do these days. Anyway, Derek couldn't see what I was doing because the plexiglass enclosure installed after Nancy's stunt obscured everything behind it. I opened it and slipped it into my back pocket.

Derek knocked on the door again. I walked toward him.

"I know you're closed, but I just need one thing," he said. "I'll be quick."

I made a show of looking at the time on my phone.

"Please," he said. "I promise. Just one thing."

Sighing, I unlocked the door. Derek slipped past me and into the darkened store.

"Thanks," he said.

"Make it fast. I'm not supposed to be here past seven-thirty and Bill doesn't pay overtime."

He disappeared down aisle three. After a few minutes, I heard the floppy doors near the meat department slam shut. So, this is how we're doing it?

How obvious. I waited a couple more minutes before calling his name. He didn't answer.

I walked through aisle three. The hairs on the back of my neck danced. I both anticipated and dreaded finding him in the back. It was anyone's guess who would win. I mean, sure I had a knife, but he might have a gun. That'd bend the odds way out of my favor. He wouldn't expect the knife, though, so maybe the element of surprise would bend shit back my way.

The excitement of not knowing made me nauseous.

I walked through the floppy doors. No Derek. Down the receiving bay toward the back door and the stairs that led down to the basement.

"Derek?" I called again. "Stop being a dick."

Nothing.

"Derek! I'll get in trouble if Bill finds out I let you in here after hours."

Not a peep from Derek. While he played right into my hands, not knowing where he was kind of annoyed me. Okay, so it scared me a little too.

Where the fuck was he?

"Derek, I'm serious now. This isn't funny."

As I stood near the basement stairs, I searched the shadows for movement. I almost turned the lights on. Derek didn't know the store as well as I did, though. I could easily find my way with the lights out. Could he?

A clatter from the basement sent a shiver over my skin. Fucker.

"Derek? I'm serious. You've gotta go. Bill comes in to do the deposit at night. I'll get in shit for letting you in if we're not gone before he comes." A lie, but Derek wouldn't know that.

Another clatter from the basement. Derek didn't emerge, though. Fine. This is how it'd be. I felt my back pocket to confirm the knife was still there and started down the stairs.

I made it almost to the staff washrooms near the back of the basement before he threw his body into me, slamming my shoulder hard against the concrete wall. The hallway to the bathrooms was narrow, with only one way out. He picked a good spot to ambush me. I had no options. Either run toward the bathrooms, with their flimsy locks and no hope of escape, or face him.

So, I faced him.

"I'm not some delicate flower, fuck-nut," I said before shoving him hard. "You won't win this fight."

He punched me twice in the face in response to my taunt. I'll confess, I was stunned enough that he was able to push me to the floor and climb on top of me. As he pulled at the button on my pants, I regained my senses. He used his knees to pin my shoulders to the floor while he unbuckled his belt. Regret for my cockiness tightened my stomach into a knot. Fear rendered me immobile for what felt like an eternity. I hated him for it, but I couldn't find the wherewithal to fight back.

I felt my pants slide down my hips, barely catching on my ass. Smelled the sweat on his skin and felt his breath on my face. He was bigger, stronger, and he could easily kill me with his bare hands if he wanted to. Probably would when he was finished.

My hands suddenly burst into action. I punched, pushed and clawed, but my efforts had little effect. Funny thing was, he said nothing. I cursed up a storm, but Derek didn't utter a single word the whole time. He grunted as I fought him, but there was no douchebag-like speech about how he knew I wanted him, or I deserve what was coming, or anything like that. It was a little unsettling. I'll admit that his strange silence sent a frisson of panic through my heart. Maybe I wouldn't make it out of this unscathed.

Finally, I swallowed the panic that weakened me, and I fought as if my life depended on it, and it did. After a few more scratches, a couple of eye-gouges, punches and kicks, I was able to lift my hips enough to reach the knife in my back pocket.

In movies, it seems easy to stab a person, but it's really not. You either get a lucky shot or you work damn hard to get the job done. I didn't get a lucky shot. I stabbed Derek several times in the stomach, the hand, the chest, but not deeply enough to make him stop. I just enraged him.

"Fucking bitch," he finally grunted before slamming me across the head with his fist.

I shook the stars from my brain and lunged at him again. A few more parlays between us, him punching, me stabbing, and the knife went through the tender skin of his throat.

He stopped punching.

I held onto the knife, two-fisting it as I pushed as hard as I could. His blood made the handle slick, and I really had to work at gripping it while he tried to escape. We retreated together on our knees until he hit the shelving next to the hallway. I heard boxes of cereal and cannisters of coffee clatter to the floor as Derek scratched at my hands. He choked, sputtered, clawed, and kicked, but I held tight, using my whole body to drive the knife into his neck as deep as it'd go. Finally, he went down, and I let go of the knife.

The rest went by in a blur. When I calmed down, I realized I couldn't remove his body. The store was too central. If I went out back, the neighbor who was always peeking out his windows would see. If I went out front, the whole town might see. I had to hide Derek in the store for now. Maybe a little planning next time wouldn't hurt.

I turned on the basement lights to assess the

damage.

The good news was his blood was limited to his clothes, my face and clothes, and the floor around him. Thank Christ for floor drains, right? Yes, absolutely right. With the mold and mildew stains on the concrete, it was almost impossible to tell what was on the floor. Almost. Only a bit of blood splattered on the walls and floor of the alcove that led to the bathroom, where someone had laid white tiles over the cement. Some industrial cleaner used by the butcher took care of that. It's not like a forensic team would be snooping around if I did the job properly anyway. I wrapped Derek in plastic and then dragged him to the stairs. When I got there, I dropped his legs. I could send him up the belt, but then where the fuck would I store him until I figured out what to do? The garage attached to the store was a cluttered mess. I could hide him in some of that, but sometimes Melanie got industrious and cleaned it out. He could be found before I had a chance to move him. I could dump him over the fence that separated the store's parking lot from the house next door, but it was too close. Someone might've seen me let him in and the cops would definitely ask questions.

I pressed my fingers against my forehead. The whole situation had me on edge. I was panicking and that would get me caught. After all that bluster about not being arrogant, here I was, guilty of the very sin that I mocked others for. Imagine thinking I was smarter than all the others who'd come before me. I didn't plan, because that implied I might be as crazy as they became, but I didn't consider that planning required logic and reason. It required someone to really think about things rationally. Of course, a little preparation ahead of the kill was the smart thing to do. My ego made me stupid and now I had a body I had no idea how to get rid of.

I knew I had to calm down or I'd fuck this all up. Closing my eyes, I took three slow, deep breaths and then glared at Derek's body. Piece of shit just wouldn't stop being a problem. Taking him upstairs was stupid. I had nowhere to stash him up there. He'd have to stay in the basement for now.

I glanced over my shoulder. No one went into the utility room unless something broke down. That happened every other week lately, though, so it wasn't a great place to store a body. It was also hot as hell in there. The smell would give Derek away in a day or two.

Next to the utility room was a large walk-in freezer used to store bakery overstock. Health codes forbade us from storing anything directly on the floor, not even in the freezers, so most of the boxes inside were set on top of skids or low make-shift tables. Eying the tables, I decided I could probably shove Derek under one of those and conceal him somehow. Yep.

That'd work.

I dragged Derek back to the scene of the crime and then removed all the boxes along the back corner of the freezer. I used the end of a broken broom handle I found in the closet next to the bathrooms to dig one of the tables free from the ice-covered floor. I dragged Derek's body inside, and very clumsily rolled him to the corner. The table covered him, but the legs weren't long enough to reach the floor with his body under it. The bakery girls would notice it was unstable and they'd discover him.

I searched the utility room until I found some floor tiles in a box under a layer of mouse shit and dust. Gagging, I brushed the top off and opened it. I removed a stack of tiles and then placed them at each end of Derek's body. The table rested on these, making it as sturdy as before, but the problem was you could clearly see the plastic.

"Fuck." I chewed the edge of my nail. Nasty habit, I know. It helped me think, though. Then I remembered I just touched mouse shit and spat and sputtered as I returned to the utility room. There, I saw the old steel bar that used to hold the loading bay closed. Rectangular in shape, about five inches wide and six feet long, it might work. I dragged it to the freezer and then laid it against the front of the table. It covered the opening and, once I dumped some frost from the back wall of the freezer over it, you might believe the bar had been there all along.

After patting myself on the back, I returned the boxes to the freezer, and kicked more ice and frost around the table and the bar, so no one would suspect the set-up hadn't been there the whole time.

You might doubt that, and maybe you're right. Maybe someone will look at what I did and say, "Hey, that wasn't there before." But if I've learned one thing working in retail, it's that no one does more than they feel they're paid to do. Minimum wage generally gets minimum effort. Not my problem is a real phrase muttered about every five minutes around here. If someone does notice something different, the work involved in digging to the bottom of that pile of boxes and removing the tables was more than minimum wage warranted, so it was almost definite whoever noticed the changes would shrug and carry on with their day, leaving Derek in his frosty grave.

If someone did find him, I would deny any knowledge. Couldn't prove anything without DNA, right? I mean, all our DNA would be in that freezer. Who could narrow the culprit down to me without a smoking gun or a confession? Speaking of the murder weapon, I decided I'd figure out where to discard the knife later. For now, I just had to get out. I quickly washed the blood from my face and hands and grabbed a new shirt from the box in the closet next to the bathrooms. I stuffed my blood-soaked shirt into a bag and then hid it in my purse.

I locked up, "forgetting" to arm the alarm so no one would know when I left and then went home. I was too charged up to sleep, though. It went so perfectly, I felt like I had to be forgetting something. I wasn't. Hiding the body in plain sight was genius and Derek didn't park in front of the store. He probably intended to rape and murder me, so he left his car at the park and walked to the store. Thanks for making my job easier, Derek. You're a true gentleman.

The Riot

The second quarantine order came down less than a week after Derek's demise, and the level of shit losing from the general public escalated well above what it was the first time. I didn't think anyone could be crazier than those toilet paper hoarding fools, but I underestimated you guys. The volume of customers and chaos in the store made moving Derek impossible.

I tried to be calm about it but ended up chewing every fingernail so far down that I drew blood. He'd given me a black eye and a fat lip that night. I quickly explained it away, saying I fell down my basement stairs. Thankfully, his assault also scraped my hands and bruised my body, so the story was believable to anyone who had no idea I was capable of murder. If anyone found him, though, my injuries didn't look so innocent anymore.

I lost a couple of nights of sleep thinking about what the worst thing that could happen would be. I mean, if someone found him, they'd never connect him to me. I'd be a suspect just like everyone else that worked at the store, but if I played it right, they'd never know for sure. On the other hand, I was the only one with two deaths linked to me, so it might be difficult to push their attention someone else's way. Maybe I'm not cut out for this killing stuff. Maybe you need to be just a little crazy to do this shit and act normal after.

"Don't invite trouble," I told myself multiple times each day. "There is no problem until there is a problem."

I kept my head down and tried to be patient with the new wave of hoarders that paraded through the doors almost immediately after the government announced the quarantine order that would take effect at noon the next day. I used every "calming" trick Google had to offer for five days. It worked. Mostly. On the sixth day, though, things went from bad to worse in the customer rage department.

"Hey," Carol from the deli said to me as I walked past the registers. "That guy is putting hamburger on the produce scales."

I looked toward the onions and sure enough, a guy had placed a package of ground beef on the scale. Jesus Christ. What was wrong with people?

"Hey!" I yelled. "You can't do that. It contaminates the scale."

The guy looked at me, saw Carol behind me, and went wild. "You fucking rat!" he screamed at Carol. "You happy now? Ratted me out, eh? Fucking rat!"

I don't know the point of his tirade, to be honest. I didn't care. He was an idiot. "She's not a rat. I *saw* you. Get the meat off the scale. The weight is on the label."

"I have to make sure you fuckers aren't cheating me," he said. "Fucking rats and thieves in here."

He removed the meat from the scale and headed toward the toilet paper aisle, ranting about rats and thieves the whole way to anyone unfortunate enough to make eye contact. I shook my head as I turned to Carol. "Get some bleach and clean that before someone uses it."

Done with all of them, I retreated from the chaos to the back room. Most of the managers had left for the day. I know, it's not the wisest decision to abandon the store with only one or two managers to keep shit under control during a quarantine order, but in their defense, we were over it. We didn't care if the whole place burned to the ground. We were done.

The idea of the store burning to the ground rolled around my head for a while. I did enjoy fire lately. Would that be a trademark? Nah, Adam's cottage was deemed an accident. No one would suspect—

"I got rotten turkey here one time," a man at the deli was saying, his shrill, nasally voice slicing through my fire daydream. "Tasted tangy. Turkey shouldn't be tangy."

I swallowed the groan that immediately leapt to my throat. This guy was in every day and told everyone about the rotten turkey he got at least two years ago. I disappeared into the back room. No way was I dealing with that asshole. He was hoping for free deli meat. We gave it to him the first couple of times he told the turkey story but got wise to it soon after. Now we just nodded and acted like we gave a shit. He also refused bags and then, after paying, said, "You know what, I need bags. Yeah, double bag it all." This was to avoid paying the five cents per bag fee. Most of the cashiers let him away with it, but I still charged him. Fuck that loser.

A scream brought me out of my turkey guy ruminating. Yelling followed and then a loud rumbling sound. Ava's voice pleaded with someone to calm down. Then the familiar ding of the speakers sounded, and I heard, "Manager to the door. Urgent. Manager to the door, *now.*"

I glanced at Mack, who paused in the task of emptying the cardboard compactor. She didn't move, but mouthed, "What now?" to me.

While I didn't want to know, I had to look. I was in charge, after all. As I emerged from the floppy doors, the scene before me unfolded in the form of a slow-motion nightmare.

Bill ran toward me, a crowd of crazies behind him. "They're out of control," he yelled as he ran past me. "No one's listening anymore."

I stood there as they tore through the produce aisle, trying (and failing) to make sense of what I saw.

Onions, fruit, and the occasional head of lettuce rolled across the floor. People punched, kicked, and bit each other as they scrambled to put as much into their carts as possible. A woman wearing one of those old-timey gas masks fell to the floor as a very round, very red man shoved her while simultaneously ripping a bag of potatoes out of her hands. The bag, being paper, didn't hold up well under this excessive level of force. It tore along the side, emptying its contents on the floor. Two women, one blonde, one redhead with white roots, ran toward the bread aisle, stepped on the potatoes, grabbed each other as though that might prevent the inevitable, and then also went down. Blood sprayed from the blonde's face as she smashed her mouth on the edge of the cheese bunker before hitting the floor.

No one stopped to see if she was okay. Hell, not a single person, aside from her friend, whose arm was bent at a concerning angle, seemed aware she even existed.

Sound seemed to stop as I watched the first few seconds of this shit show, and I realized Bill left us. He fucking *left us*!

Suddenly, the audio caught up with the visuals, and I heard a man call someone a greedy fuck, and then the sound of so many cans hitting the floor. A crash followed. I was pretty sure a shelf got knocked over. While all of this was concerning, my brain couldn't let go of one thought:

Bill fucking left.

Mother fucker.

Now, you might think a riot is unlikely in a town as small as ours. I sure did. When you push people past common sense, as this fucking plague has done, a riot is inevitable, even in Hicksville.

When people get to this point, there's no reasoning with them. There's no calming them down or taking control of the situation. Also, I earned minimum wage and the owner cared so much that he abandoned us. That made this someone else's circus and monkeys. So, instead of rushing in to break them up, I backed through the floppy doors and picked up the phone to call the cashier working Lane One.

"Hello?" she shrieked.

"I want all of you in the back now," I said. "Treat it like a fire and evacuate."

"But we have to cash people out."

Glass shattered somewhere and I heard a loud bang. "No. They're past that."

"But Bill will—"

"Bill just fucked off, so screw him. Get everyone to the back. Now. It's not safe to keep working."

I hung up the phone and then lifted it up again to do a page. "All staff to receiving," I said. "All staff to receiving. Now."

Slowly, my coworkers pushed their way to the back. I waited until I was sure everyone made it and then ordered them all outside.

"We can't leave," Leah said. "They're going to take everything."

"They're doing it anyway," Hal argued. "I don't make enough to try to stop them either."

"Should we call the cops?" Mack asked.

"I did," I lied. I couldn't call yet. This whole shit show gave me the perfect way to dispose of Derek and I wasn't missing the opportunity. "You guys wait here for the cops. I'm going to check the other door."

"Why?" Leah asked.

"To make sure it's not barred. Don't want to trap anyone in here." I didn't care if anyone got trapped, as you've probably guessed. I just needed an excuse to light another match.

I walked around the building. As I passed Hal's truck, I saw a gas can in the back. Fire was becoming a theme for me. Boring? Maybe. Predictable too. Yes, I might be treading dangerously close to a trademark by setting two fires but needs must. Hey, if it ain't broke, right?

I picked up the can. Almost full. As I walked inside, the commotion on the sales floor had grown to an almost deafening level. The ping-ping of cans hitting the floor blended into the melody of glass shattering and people screaming in rage, fear, and excitement. Curses flew alongside the cries of pain, punctuated by the sound of shoes squeaking against the tile floor.

By the way, chaos has a smell. I didn't realize this until the pandemic happened, but it really does. It's hard to describe. Sort of like something hot, almost burning, yet cold at the same time. In between, there's something sour. Like the smell of the first snow...only someone burned garbage right before.

While I wanted to assess the damage, I had limited time to do what needed to be done, so I didn't bother to investigate. Instead, I ran downstairs to the freezers in the basement. I trashed the place uncovering Derek's corpse. It took some tugging to get him out of his spot, the plastic ripped as some of it stayed frozen to the cement floor. No big deal. I just needed his body.

After dragging him out, I laid him near the shelves of cereal. These would go up fast and they'd take him with them. I poured gas on Derek and on the boxes and then I took the lighter out of my pocket and set fire to a box on the end of the shelves. It caught quickly and I ran with my gas can back up the stairs. I poured gas all over the back and then shook the remaining drops out the floppy doors on the floor near the meat department.

Think. Think. Think.

I glanced through the doors and saw smoke billowing out of aisle five. Someone else set the store on fire. The universe loved me. That much was clear.

I ran out the back door, dramatically coughing and sputtering.

"Hey!" Hal yelled as he jogged toward me. "What's going on?"

"They set it on fire!" I said. "I couldn't see if everyone got out. I tried, but—"

"All the staff is accounted for," Hal said. "Fuck the rest of them. Crazy assholes want to start a riot, they deserve whatever happens to them."

Amen, Hal.

We heard sirens and backed away from the building. By the time the firetrucks arrived, the whole place was ablaze. They pushed us all back and we watched as our jobs went up in smoke.

I don't think any of us gave a shit.

The Epilogue

We became famous because of the riot and the fire that ended it. On the bright side, only two people died as a result; rotten turkey man, who got trampled during the panicked escape from the flames, and Derek. Staff was interviewed by the cops, the fire Marshall, and several national news services. We were ordered by Corporate to decline media interviews but fuck them. We all made sure the world knew of the unacceptable conditions we had to work in, without them offering a single dime in compensation. It made such a stir on the Internet that Corporate ended up paying us full wages while the store was rebuilt.

We also filed a lawsuit. That'll take years to work out, though.

During the months spent rebuilding the store, I wrote this story. I'm happy to report I've had no desire to kill anyone since the fire. Probably because most of the deadbeats in this town calmed down after nearly dying, and (if I'm honest) no one has had a chance to piss me off. We were on lockdown for four weeks, during which time the fire was "thoroughly" investigated and then blamed on the looters, and Derek's murder believed to be some kind of "retribution" by an unknown assailant involved with the riot.

Pretty fucking perfect if you ask me. During my first week back to work, nothing could dampen my good spirits, but then I asked Kendall and Melanie to read this manuscript. Their reaction was underwhelming.

"This all happened," Melanie said. "I mean, all these things except maybe Jolene, but she hasn't been seen in..."

"So? Authors use real events all the time."

"But it looks like you're confessing."

I laughed. "Hardly. I couldn't kill someone."

"I know that, but this will be read by people who don't know you. They're going to think you did all of this."

She made a good point. "So, I just change names and some of the details. Think it's good enough to be published?"

"Jesus Christ," Kendall said. "Why would you want to publish it?"

"I dunno," I said. "I always wanted to write a book, I guess."

"But most of this stuff actually happened."

"Yeah, Melanie pointed that out already and I said I'd change names, dates, and places. Don't you like it?"

"It's good. I mean, I couldn't put it down, but I

don't know if I'd publish it."

I shouldn't draw attention to myself. I know that. If they found Jolene, these two would remember what they read, and I'd be fucked. They were already turning on me and they just thought I had bad judgment. If they went away, though... No. They were good people. That would go against my code. Also, I'd have to add chapters and I like the book the way it is.

"I'll use a pen name," I said. "And maybe I'll take out the bit about the riot?"

"I don't know," Melanie replied. "It's just... It'd be hard for you to explain."

Okay, now she was pissing me off. Mostly because she made sense. I know I should just leave it alone. I mean, I'm not even close to finished and every serial killer gets caught because they eventually want credit for their work. The book, in a small way, is kind of letting me have some glory for my accomplishments. It did smell a little bit like bragging. When killers do that, they get caught, but I'm not like every other killer. Am I?

No, I'm smarter.

Fire is not my trademark. This book is not a confession. I will not kill these two because they're Debbie Downers. Maybe I should set the manuscript aside, see what shakes out as life goes back to normal. I may have to start a second book, and it'd probably be better to hand the publisher a finished product, rather than just a single instalment.

Yes…

Retail, the series…

Brilliant.

As long as I don't get caught.

Printed in Great Britain
by Amazon